"Can you explain how we're still married, Kate?

"I signed and mailed the divorce papers."

"I know," she whispered. "But I never received the documents to sign on my end."

"You're telling me the divorce paperwork was lost in the mail?"

Biting her lip, she nodded. "My attorney's son called to let me know. He realized our case had fallen through the cracks."

Jack gritted his teeth. "What real difference does it make? We were broken long before this."

"The divorce wasn't the only reason that brought me stateside. There were other matters I needed to attend to." She looked away. "I need to make my peace with the past."

"You came home for Liddy."

"I've had no home since Liddy… Since you and I…"

He knew exactly what she meant.

She raised her gaze. "I'm not sure I can face it."

Perhaps by helping her, he could also help himself better accept the worst thing that ever happened to either of them. Jack took a deep breath. "We'll face the anniversary together. You won't be alone through this. I promise you."

Lisa Carter and her family make their home in North Carolina. In addition to her Love Inspired novels, she writes romantic suspense. When she isn't writing, Lisa enjoys traveling to romantic locales, teaching writing workshops and researching her next exotic adventure. She has strong opinions on barbecue and ACC basketball. She loves to hear from readers. Connect with Lisa at lisacarterauthor.com.

Books by Lisa Carter

Love Inspired

Coast Guard Courtship
Coast Guard Sweetheart
Falling for the Single Dad
The Deputy's Perfect Match
The Bachelor's Unexpected Family
The Christmas Baby
Hometown Reunion
His Secret Daughter
The Twin Bargain
Stranded for the Holidays
The Christmas Bargain
A Chance for the Newcomer
A Safe Place for Christmas
Reclaiming the Rancher's Heart

K-9 Companions

Finding Her Way Back

Visit the Author Profile page at LoveInspired.com.

Reclaiming the Rancher's Heart

Lisa Carter

LOVE INSPIRED

INSPIRATIONAL ROMANCE

LOVE INSPIRED®

INSPIRATIONAL ROMANCE

Recycling programs for this product may not exist in your area.

ISBN-13: 978-1-335-58546-2

Reclaiming the Rancher's Heart

Copyright © 2022 by Lisa Carter

For questions and comments about the quality of this book, please contact us at CustomerService@Harlequin.com.

Love Inspired
22 Adelaide St. West, 41st Floor
Toronto, Ontario M5H 4E3, Canada
www.LoveInspired.com

Printed in U.S.A.

In all these things we are more than conquerors through him that loved us. For I am persuaded, that neither death, nor life, nor angels, nor principalities, nor powers, nor things present, nor things to come, Nor height, nor depth, nor any other creature, shall be able to separate us from the love of God, which is in Christ Jesus our Lord.

—*Romans* 8:37–39

To my grandmother,
who lost three young children during a
terrible eighteen-month period from 1931 to 1932.
And to all the mothers who've faced this
most devastating of losses.

This book is especially dedicated to the
handful of bereaved mothers I've had the
privilege to call friend. You know who you are.
Through the years, I've prayed for you often. My
heart hurts with yours in this deepest of sorrows.
You are the bravest women I know. I love you.

Chapter One

Coming out of the barn, when Jack caught sight of her standing by the pasture fence, he froze midstep.

In that first, startled split second, a joy so sweet as to be nearly indescribable flashed through him. But then aching remembrance lacerated his heart. A devastating pain. The drowning sorrow. Suffocating guilt.

He couldn't move. His heart, or what passed for it these days, pounded. He couldn't breathe.

After three years of silence, she'd made it clear he had no right to feel anything for her. He shouldn't feel anything for her. Yet the habit of loving her tugged at him like an unseen but inescapable riptide.

Overturning his hard-won peace. Pulling him out on a sea of regret. Dragging him under the waves of darkness. His fist clenched around the bridle trailing in the dust beneath his boots.

"Jack?" Her hazel eyes clouding, she took a step toward him and stopped. "Say something."

A thousand thoughts buzzed through his head. Jumbled emotions that had churned his brain during a thousand sleepless nights. So many accusations he'd burned to lob at her. But at the moment of opportunity, the words evaporated from his tongue. Dissipating like the morning mist on the mountain. Deserting him just as she once had, too.

Leaving in their place the one thing that had kept him on his feet, fighting to live through another bleak day without her.

"What have we got left to say to each other, Kate?" He jutted his jaw. "Unless there was something you forgot to tell me in the goodbye note you left on the nightstand." He laughed, a sound without mirth. "Oh, wait. That's right. There was no note. You left without a word. Until I heard from your lawyer, that is."

Her lips trembled. "I'm sorry."

No words existed to express how sorry he was. Although he tried over and over that terrible summer three years ago.

A breeze played with the long, wavy tendrils of her red-gold hair. His beautiful, beautiful Kate. She appeared thinner than when he last saw her. Pale and slightly hollow-cheeked, dark shadows bruised her eyes.

Still beautiful, but no longer his.

"I'm d—" Biting her lip, her liquid gaze flitted across the bucolic scene of horses grazing in the pasture. "I was in such pain."

Jack's nostrils flared. "And I wasn't?"

Her eyes snapped to his. "If I could go back and change what happened…"

Jack swallowed, hard. "Wouldn't we both."

Nearly unsettling his Stetson, he scrubbed his hand over his face to clear his vision. If only the last three years could be so easily erased. But the dead couldn't be made undead. Nor could their marriage. And what they'd once meant to each other.

He hunched his shoulders. The all-too-familiar, hopeless fatigue settled over him again. A burden, which only in the last year had he begun to throw off. "If that's all you've come for…"

"Jack."

He closed his eyes against the raw pain in her voice. Her torment shredded his insides. "Why are you here?"

Somewhere under a bush near the farmhouse, a thrush was singing its heart out.

"We have…unfinished business."

His eyes flew open, narrowing on her. "That's the interesting thing about divorce, Kate. It finishes everything."

"Did it?" She lifted her chin. "Finalize everything?"

"I don't understand."

There was something in her face… Something he couldn't pinpoint. He'd made a career of trusting his instincts. Those instincts had saved his life and his team on more than one war-torn operation. Something was off. She was off.

"It's almost the three-year anniversary."

He gritted his teeth. "I haven't forgotten." *Would that he could.* "Why have you finally come back now?"

She flinched.

"After three long years of keeping vigil alone—" his voice and his temper rose "—of grave-tending alone… Now you feel ready?"

Her eyes sparked. "I buried my heart in that cemetery, Jack Dolan. I'll never be ready, but ready or not, time's run out."

What did that mean?

"Yours wasn't the only heart broken, Kate Breckenridge." His lips twisted. "I assume you dropped the Dolan as fast as you dropped me."

"Don't." She folded her arms across her chest. "Please, Jack. Let's not tear each other apart again."

"Why not?" He made to move past her. "It's about the only thing we do well."

She laid her hand on his arm. "That's not the only thing we did well."

Tingles of awareness shot up his arm. Spearing what was left of his heart. Her eyes widened. She'd felt it, too. She dropped her hold on him.

But the indisputable fact that the touch of her hand could still affect his equilibrium made him angry. Furious. Making a mockery of his dearly fought battle to move on with his life. To let go of her. To lay to rest everything that had been before.

Yet here she was, reopening old wounds. And inflicting new ones.

"What do you want from me, Kate?"

"I want—" Her face constricted. She took a shuddery breath. "It—it doesn't matter what I want. But I'd settle for peace." The reddish tints in her hair glinted in the midmorning sun.

His gaze swung to the picture-perfect blue sky over the mountain ridge. Peace is what he'd believed he had until she showed up today. Now emptiness swelled inside his chest, threatening to swallow him whole.

"I wish you well with that." He turned away. "I really do."

If he didn't walk away right this minute, he would say something he shouldn't. Do something he mustn't. Lose himself once more. He never wanted to be that broken again.

He strode past her toward the farmhouse. Fighting to regulate his breathing, he clomped up the porch steps. He gripped the bridle like an anchor. Or a lifeline.

The symbol of his new life. Pulling him back from the brink of despair. Halting his downward spiral. The horse ranch had saved his sanity.

God had saved everything else.

Kate watched the hard line of his broad shoulders under the cotton shirt as he walked away. Her vision blurred. She deserved his anger. She'd hurt him. They'd hurt each other. And yet…

She inhaled sharply. It was so good to see him. Taking a slight edge off the constant pain that lived inside her since the accident destroyed their lives.

His dark hair had grown out of the military cut he'd worn throughout their marriage when he was in Special Forces. It was a little longer. A little shaggier. The way he'd worn it when they were teenagers.

The younger seventeen-year-old Kate had been drawn to him. Drawn to the hint of the rebel that called to something inside her. She'd been pulled like a magnet to that cowboy swagger of his. To the something that made Jack Dolan so beguiling to her. Then as now, he was still so dangerous to her peace of mind.

When he'd walked out of the barn, goose bumps had frolicked across her skin like ladybugs. Seeing him today did funny things to her heart. The door on the screened porch of the farmhouse banged shut behind him. She jerked.

They'd met when he was barely more than a boy, and she had only just begun to believe she'd survive her bout with childhood cancer. The adolescent Jack had affected her much the same way as the thirty-three-year-old Jack did still.

Fifteen years ago. Such a happy, sunny June morning. Not unlike today. She sighed. A June so very unlike today.

Her attention wandered to the pasture where they'd met all those years ago. The never-to-be-forgotten moment their gazes locked. Mirrored in his startling blue eyes, she'd glimpsed a reflection of herself. But more than that. She'd seen hope for a future. Together.

And she'd been able to put a name to the ache she'd felt her entire life. The ache only Jack Dolan had ever been able to fill.

Those eyes of his...

She headed to the rental car, parked on the gravel drive in front of the white farmhouse. Those eyes of his haunted her dreams. His eyes and swimming pools.

A sudden chill assailed her. She got in the car, closing the door in her mind on that horrible day three years ago. Coming to the ranch this morning had been a mistake. Reviving old memories best left buried.

Pulling away, she glanced in the rearview mirror. She half expected Jack's grandmother to come rushing out like an avenging warrior. CoraFaye had never been her biggest fan.

Last night, Kate returned unannounced to Truelove. She wasn't sure why her first stop this morning had been to see Jack. She frowned.

Not true.

She brought so many secrets with her. *At least be honest with yourself.* She knew exactly why she'd come this morning.

Kate steered onto the secondary road that led over the mountain toward the small Blue Ridge town.

She'd come because there'd always been this inexplicable cord binding her and Jack. An irresistible force. The tragedy had cut deeply into the connection they shared, but after this morning's encounter, it appeared nothing could completely sever it.

Would death?

She'd set out to see him this morning. She couldn't *not* see him. Not if they were remotely in the same hemisphere. Certainly not when she was in Truelove. Back where they began.

Life—*what an irony*—had come full circle.

The car hugged the road, winding around the mountain like a corkscrew. Pink rhododendron and white mountain laurel dotted the slopes of the evergreen-studded Blue Ridge. On the other side of the thin, metal guardrail, the land dropped away into a gorge.

Her hands tightened on the wheel. Three years ago, she'd wanted to die. Begged God to take her. When He didn't, when she could no longer bear the chasm of mutual recrimination between her and Jack, she'd fled to Africa.

She lost herself in her work. Desperate for a purpose beyond her pain. A reason to get up each morning.

Now finally—another irony—God had seen fit to answer her prayer. She should've been more careful what she prayed for.

Descending into the valley, she emerged into gentler terrain. Orchards with groves of leafed-out apple trees lined both sides of the road. Farther along, she drove past fields studded with newly mown hay.

Within a matter of minutes, she reached the outskirts of Truelove. She jolted as the car clattered over the bridge. The gushing river below formed a horseshoe around the town limits.

Not much had changed in Truelove since Liddy's death. There was a timeless quality to the tiny hamlet. On the horizon, wave upon wave of undulating, blue-green ridges enfolded the charming town. Promising a slower pace of life. The simplicity and goodness of small things.

She was due to meet her grandmother for an early lunch at the Mason Jar Café. But feeling suddenly nostalgic, she decided to take a quick five-cent tour. She steered around the town square.

Gram had kept her relentlessly informed of the neighborly happenings via long letters written in flowing script on lavender-scented sheets of ivory stationery.

In the middle of the village green, she spotted what remained of the historic gazebo, destroyed in a spring tornado several years ago, but scheduled for restoration. A sure indicator that time stood still for no one. No matter how much she wanted to rewind the clock.

To three summers ago. Further even. To the time she met Jack, when life had seemed an eternal summer. But there was no going back. No do-overs. Scarred by loss, she and Jack were different people.

She veered into an empty parking space along the curb outside the café. Another sign of change. Gram had said the eatery was under new ownership. When Kate jerked open the glass-fronted door, a bell jangled overhead.

Inside the café, the delectable aroma of ground coffee beans and the yeasty smell of pastry floated past her nostrils. She sniffed appreciably. Perhaps all change wasn't necessarily bad.

Jam-packed, the restaurant sported a classy French bistro vibe. Southern comfort food meets Paris. Despite her morning, she couldn't help but smile at the flurry of activity in the cheery café. Refilling coffee mugs and delivering trays laden with orders, waitresses scurried from booth to booth.

Hearing her name, she turned away from her contemplation of the cherry red stools lining the long, white counter. Seated at the large table underneath the bulletin board, Gram beckoned her. But recognizing the cluster of older women with her grandmother, Kate's heart sank.

Pasting a too-bright smile on her features, she moved toward them. "Gram." She planted a quick kiss on her grandmother's soft cheek. "You should've told me you already had plans with your friends in the Double Name Club."

Behind the clear, wire-rimmed spectacles, Gram's cornflower blue eyes twinkled. "Must've slipped my mind."

She doubted the likelihood of that. A retired librarian, her grandmother had a mind like a steel trap. And Kate's thoughts on the Double Name Club—more notoriously known as the Truelove Matchmakers—were best left unvoiced.

The ladies were infamous for poking their powdered noses where they didn't belong. They took the town motto—*Truelove, Where True Love Awaits*—a little too seriously.

She and Jack had been only too happy to become one of their little matchmaking projects. *And look how well that turned out.*

Never-met-a-stranger ErmaJean Hicks clapped her plump hands together. "Just our usual Friday lunch get-together."

"And the gang's all here." Kate gritted her teeth. "I don't want to interrupt, Miss ErmaJean."

Married, divorced or spinster, any Southern lady who was your elder had the honorary title of respect, "Miss," bestowed on her. Whether elderly or not.

"Nonsense." GeorgeAnne Allen, the uncontested leader of the matchmaker pack, grunted. "We left a chair for you."

Faintly terrifying with ice-blue eyes and a short, iron-gray cap of hair, GeorgeAnne was the bossy one. Although when it came to the Double Name Club, that was splitting hairs.

ErmaJean smiled. "When we heard Marth'Alice's granddaughter was in town, we were so delighted for the chance to see you again."

Kate couldn't help but smile at the drawled-out, honeyed, North Carolina version of Gram's given name, Martha Alice.

The oldest and most diminutive member of the club, IdaLee, gestured to the empty chair next to the only other occupant of the table besides Kate under seventy. "I don't believe you've met AnnaBeth."

Smiling, the stylishly dressed woman fluttered her fingers at Kate. And she suddenly recalled Gram mentioning the attractive redhead, who'd found herself stranded in Truelove one Christmas a few years ago.

IdaLee's snow-white hair in the schoolmarm bun glistened under the café lights. "AnnaBeth married my great-nephew Jonas. Do you remember him?"

She did. Jonas Stone, owner of a local dude ranch, was Jack's cousin on their dads' side. Gazing at the women's upturned faces, she bit off a sigh. There was no getting out of it. Like death and taxes, she accepted the inevitability of the coming interrogation and pulled out the chair.

The café had always been Operation Central in the Truelove grapevine. The matchmakers didn't mean any real harm. She hoped Southern niceties of politeness, culturally ingrained since birth, would prevent them from bringing up the elephant in the room—Jack.

And she prayed—something she hadn't done in a long time—that human compassion would prevent them from expressing well-meaning condolences.

One of the reasons she'd fled three years ago. When

she could no longer bear phrases like *unimaginable loss, unbearable grief, unfathomable pain.*

She sat down. "I hear congratulations are in order, Miss IdaLee, for your Christmas wedding last year." *Thank you, Gram, for supplying that distracting conversational tidbit.*

IdaLee blushed like a schoolgirl. "Charles and I eloped."

AnnaBeth Stone smiled. "So romantic."

"Yet nothing beats a spring garden wedding." GeorgeAnne arched her brow. "I'm sure you would agree, wouldn't you, Kate?"

She felt a rush of heat creep from beneath the collar of her shirt. She and Jack had gotten married in Gram's garden. And yes, it had been romantic. Until their dream marriage became a nightmare of regret.

AnnaBeth's emerald green eyes sparkled. "I've been looking forward to meeting you, Kate."

Obviously, the matchmakers hadn't told AnnaBeth about Kate's story. Jonas's wife looked to be a few years younger than her and Jack. She pressed her lips together. Why did everything, every thought, always have to come back to him?

The conversation swung to other items of community interest. The awkward moment passed. Gram asked AnnaBeth about the latest post on her *Heart's Home* blog. A social media influencer, AnnaBeth had a national following.

IdaLee teased her lifelong friends, GeorgeAnne and ErmaJean, about their own not-so-young gentlemen callers. Kate glanced at her grandmother. A spot of color peppered Gram's porcelain cheeks. Did her grandmother have her own gentleman caller? What hadn't Gram mentioned in those letters about herself?

Catching her gaze, Gram's lips quirked. "We should probably order." Her long, slim fingers touched her elegant, silvery 'do. "I've got my standing Friday shampoo and set at Hair Raisers this afternoon."

At the same moment ErmaJean lifted her hand to signal the waitress, the bell above the entrance jangled furiously. Heads turned. CoraFaye Dolan stalked across the café toward them.

"You!" The thick, single braid of salt-and-pepper hair hanging down CoraFaye's back fairly quivered with outrage. "Aren't you supposed to be in Africa tending to people who need you?"

The background din of pleasant conversation ground to an immediate halt.

In her sixties, the older woman curled her lip. "Nobody needs or wants you here, Princess."

Gram bristled. "You wait right there, CoraFaye Dolan."

She laid her hand on her grandmother's arm. "Don't," she whispered.

"I 'bout wore out my knees praying over that boy when he joined the Navy." CoraFaye planted her scrawny hands on her jean-clad hips. "And through those can't-discuss-it-SEAL missions. Off for weeks at a time. In harm's way. God alone knowing where."

After Jack was orphaned young, his grandmother had practically raised him. Kate had lost her own parents, too. Their shared, early losses had drawn them together. As surely as their last loss tore them apart.

ErmaJean's mouth trembled. "Please don't do this, Cora-Faye."

"This is not the place." IdaLee's lips tightened. "Nor the time."

CoraFaye shook her finger in Kate's face. "But it wasn't

the Taliban. Or war. Or anything else that nearly put an end to him."

Her heart thundered. Spots danced before her eyes. She had to get out of here. *Now.* She pushed back her chair. She cringed as the chair scraped across the linoleum.

The sound felt inordinately loud, jarring. Setting her head to pounding. She fought a crashing wave of dizziness. She gripped the edge of the table to steady herself. She couldn't have another attack. Not in front of everyone.

"It was you, Kate Breckenridge." Behind the black, cat's-eye glasses, CoraFaye's blue eyes—so like Jack's—blazed. "And here you are turning up like a bad penny just when he's begun to find happiness once more. Putting his life together again. The life you did your best to ruin."

"You're not the only one who lost a great-grandchild, CoraFaye." Gram surged to her feet. "You better take hold of your baby sister, GeorgeAnne. Before I forget I'm a Christian woman and smack her down a peg or two." She shook her knitting tote over the table in the air between them.

GeorgeAnne pulled at Jack's irate grandmother. "Stop it, CoraFaye."

In the way of many families of their generation, the two sisters were separated by over a decade in age. Like so many women in the Blue Ridge descended from the Scots-Irish, physically the two of them represented both ends of the genetic spectrum. GeorgeAnne, like Kate herself, was tall and angular. CoraFaye, petite and wiry.

Yet no matter the size, feisty was a cultural given.

The other women rose, including AnnaBeth. Kate could only imagine what the young woman must think of her. Then her eyes fell to AnnaBeth's softly rounded belly. Her breath hitched.

Gram hadn't mentioned in her last letter AnnaBeth and Jonas Stone were expecting their first child. As a nurse-midwife with advanced certification, Kate thought it was ridiculous that the sight of a pregnant woman should pierce her so. But it did. Even though she'd continued to deliver babies in remote villages in Africa.

The bell jangled again. GeorgeAnne and CoraFaye blocked her view of which unsuspecting soul had wandered into this lunch fiasco. Best show in town. No one had bothered to lower their voices. This is what passed for entertainment in sleepy Truelove.

"A millstone around his neck," CoraFaye ranted. "I thank God every day Jack's no longer married to you."

Equally furious, headache forgotten, Kate drew up. Pushing back against everything taken from her. "Wrong again, CoraFaye. As it turns out, Jack and me..." Smirking, she flipped her hair over her shoulder. "We're still married."

The collective gasp ricocheted across the restaurant. Blinking, CoraFaye stumbled back a step. And Kate's first glimpse of the latest Mason Jar arrival sucked the oxygen from her lungs.

Jack rocked on his heels. "What are you talking about, Kate?"

Chapter Two

The ensuing silence felt deafening.

Horrified at what she'd let slip, Kate went hot, then cold. She'd been goaded by CoraFaye, but that was no excuse. This was not how she'd meant to tell Jack that in the eyes of the law, they were still technically married.

In the last week since coming face-to-face with her own mortality and her resolve to finally confront the past, she hadn't even decided if she *would* tell him.

But as Jack's deceased grandfather would've said, there was no use shutting the barn door after the horse had bolted.

A variety of emotions flitted across Jack's chiseled features. Shock. Anger. And something she wasn't sure how to interpret.

"You're lying," CoraFaye hissed, her lips flattening.

Such a sweet man, Jack's grandfather. The polar opposite of his control-freak wife. Kate's stomach churned. She feared she might vomit. One of the more recent and troubling symptoms.

"I'm not lying," she whispered through clenched teeth.

What CoraFaye thought of her didn't matter. It had only ever mattered what Jack thought of her.

But a stoic look fell over his features. The one he'd worn when leaving for an undisclosed mission. The shutting-her-out look.

Compartmentalizing his feelings was how he mentally survived what he experienced as a Special Forces operator. After Liddy's death, she'd been all over the place emotionally. And she'd envied him the coping mechanism.

"I—I…" Her voice hitched. "I can explain." She took a step toward him.

He tugged his quivering grandmother to his side, tucking her underneath his arm. "I'm sure you can. You always do."

An expression of sheer stubbornness had overtaken his stoicism. A stubbornness she used to be able to soothe away with feather-light kisses along his square jawline.

"But this time, you don't get to dictate the terms of where and when we have that conversation. I'll call you." The glance he threw her way was hard. "When *I'm* ready. Maybe after I talk to my own lawyer first."

She felt it like a blow to her solar plexus. She'd lost him. Lost the ability to reach him. She saw it now. And it rocked her world as it hadn't been rocked since she beheld the limp, dripping-wet body of her baby in his strong arms.

Kate staggered.

Yet what had she expected in returning to Truelove? How did she expect him to react after everything that happened between them? She was such a fool.

He marched his grandmother past the gaping bystanders, rubbernecking at the café calamity. Bell clanging like a wind chime in a hurricane, he thrust open the door and walked out. A tall blonde slipped out behind them.

Through the plate-glass windows overlooking the green, she watched him help CoraFaye into the Dolans' old Chevy pickup. He spoke to the blonde woman at his elbow.

CoraFaye had accused her of returning just as Jack had finally begun to find happiness again. Apparently, Kate hadn't been the only one meeting someone for lunch at the Mason Jar.

Her knees buckled and gave way underneath her. She began a slow, silent glide to the floor.

Quickly, AnnaBeth cupped Kate's elbow, halting her descent. "Miss Marth'Alice, why don't I drive Kate to your house. Maybe one of y'all can pick me up there and bring me back for my car."

She found herself handing over her car keys to Anna-Beth. Shame smote her. Nurse-midwives should be made of sterner stuff. But in the hullabaloo of nearly fainting in a day awash with humiliation, she completely missed what happened between Jack and the blonde. By the time AnnaBeth tucked her into her parked rental, Jack and the woman were gone.

"I'm not sure you heard." Driving south on Main, past City Hall and the police department, AnnaBeth flicked a glance at Kate. "Miss Marth'Alice said she'd come home as soon as she canceled her appointment at Hair Raisers."

Closing her eyes, Kate groaned. "And thus I've managed to singlehandedly break a standing tradition of forty-plus years."

"Your grandmother's glad that you've come home."

She opened her eyes. "I can't imagine why."

AnnaBeth steered into her grandmother's neighborhood, a five-minute drive from downtown. Nothing was very far from anywhere in tiny Truelove. Even the outlying areas—like the FieldStone Dude Ranch or Jack's horse farm—were at most only twenty minutes away.

"I'm so sorry to have inconvenienced you." Against

her will, her gaze fell to the unmistakable bump in Anna-Beth's belly. Her training kicked in. "It's not good for you to miss lunch."

"Aunt IdaLee will make sure I get something." Anna-Beth waved at someone walking a tiny Chihuahua on the sidewalk. "Jonas and I are thrilled. Not that I don't already love Jonas's son, Hunter, as my own, of course." A line furrowed her brow, and she gave Kate a quick look. "It's just this is our first baby together."

She fought the urge to wince. AnnaBeth truly didn't know about her history. She wasn't sure if she was grateful the older women hadn't gossiped about her, or if she preferred everything had already been laid out on the table for public consumption.

AnnaBeth drove past the stately, Colonial Revival homes. The houses in this section of Truelove had been built in the 1920s and 1930s. A slightly more upscale area where folks like the mayor lived. Until his retirement, Granddad had been an administrator at the nearby liberal arts college, Ashmont.

Which meant nothing to her grandparents or Kate, but had proved yet another bone of contention between herself and CoraFaye. Jack's grandparents, like the Dolan generations before them, were ranchers and farmers. From the tough Blue Ridge soil, they'd scraped out a more hardscrabble life.

"Truth to tell…" AnnaBeth pulled into the driveway and parked in the half circle in front of the Breckenridge house.

Kate turned in the seat, giving the younger mom-to-be her full attention.

"I've had weight insecurities my entire life." As if ashamed to face Kate, AnnaBeth didn't—wouldn't—look at her. "I'm so happy about this baby, but at the same time anxious about what it's doing to my body."

Kate would've never guessed that about the poised woman. AnnaBeth exuded confidence and sophistication.

"For years, I've struggled not to equate body image with love. After I met Jonas... He's been wonderful." AnnaBeth gripped the wheel. "I feel like I'm already as big as a house and still a month to go. Suppose when he looks at me, he..." Tears pooled in her brilliant green eyes.

Kate laid her hand over AnnaBeth's on the wheel. "I've known Jonas Stone since we were teenagers." Nearly as long as she'd known Jack. "Jonas is a good man."

So was Jack. And yet how despicably she'd abandoned him.

"When Jonas sees you and the baby, he will only love you more. Just like Jack—" She bit the inside of her cheek.

AnnaBeth gazed at her for a long moment. "I don't know what happened to you and Jack. I don't need to know. But if you ever need a friend in Truelove, I'm a good listener. I won't judge."

She felt the sting of tears. "Thank you." She didn't deserve such kindness.

AnnaBeth squeezed her hand. Her gaze flicked to the rearview mirror. "Looks like my ride is here, and Miss Marth'Alice is right behind Miss ErmaJean."

They got out of the rental. AnnaBeth called a final goodbye. The bay to the garage opened, and Kate's grandmother steered her town car inside. ErmaJean and Anna-Beth drove away.

Kate hesitated before following Gram into the house. Her grandmother could read her so well. Better than anyone, except Jack. She'd have to be careful around Gram.

Not yet ready to face her grandmother, she took a quick detour through the gate into Gram's garden.

As for Jack?

Her heart twisted. He wanted nothing to do with her. He'd made that only too clear. Having to avoid him wouldn't be an issue.

"Did you know about this still-married thing, Jack?" At the ranch, his grandma paced the length of the living room. "It can't be true. Can it?"

Stunned, he stared unseeing out the window at the wildflower-studded meadow. Seeing there a younger version of himself and Kate the summer when he first kissed—

"Jack!"

He swung around.

Working into a fine head of steam, his grandmother sat on the sofa and then stood up again, unable to settle. "She's lyin'. You signed paperwork, didn't you?"

He scrubbed his hand over his face. Kate was many things. But she was not a liar.

"Are you listening to me?" Grandma clutched his sleeve. "I remember you signed a bunch of legal documents. You mailed them to that fancy lawyer of hers."

He gazed beyond her to the dining room. Two years ago, he sat at the table and signed away not only his marriage but his hope, too.

Jack had spent the better part of the last two years wrestling through that, although God might hate divorce, He had only love and compassion for those who found themselves there.

He and Kate had been young when they married, but he'd had the beautiful example of his parents and grandparents to follow. He'd gone into marriage believing he and Kate would be together forever.

Tromping back and forth in front of the mantel, his grandmother continued her tirade.

Yet as he'd carried the lifeless body of his child out of the water, hadn't a small part of him known his marriage would also die?

A few weeks later, he hadn't been that surprised to return from a team meeting on the base near Virginia Beach to find Kate gone from their apartment. After the tense, dark silence between them, it was almost a relief the other shoe he'd been expecting had finally dropped.

He didn't go after her. And he didn't fight her when he was served divorce papers. He lost the right to Kate's love when he allowed their two-year-old daughter to drown. He deserved every bad thing that happened to him.

"You need to go over there right now." Grandma pointed in the general direction of Truelove. "Set that woman straight. She's brought nothing but trouble to your life." His grandmother wagged her bony finger in his face. "I rue the day you ever met her."

"Lay off Kate, Grandma."

Unbidden images flitted through his mind. Of the summer day they met. Their wedding. The birth of Liddy.

Despite how things ended, Kate had brought so much love and joy to his life. Beautiful moments he'd never trade, even if he'd known the sorrow to come.

Grandma threw out her hands. "Kate Breckenridge is toxic. Absolutely tox— Where are you going?"

Jack headed for the door. "I'm not going to discuss Kate with you." He never had. He wasn't about to start now.

"She's unreliable. You can't trust her," his grandmother shouted.

He yanked open the screen door and let it slam shut behind him.

Out in the yard, gravel crunched beneath his boots. Chest heaving, he threw himself into the truck. Was it true? Were he and Kate still legally married?

Hadn't he sensed she was holding something back this morning outside the barn? What was her real reason for returning to Truelove? To visit Liddy's grave? To get him to sign papers again? Or both?

Jack gripped the wheel. Grandma was right about one thing. No point in second-guessing how to proceed until he talked to his ex—

Wait. Kate wasn't his ex-wife. His heart lurched in his chest. She was his wife. How had it happened they were still married?

He cranked the engine and shifted into gear. Time to find some answers. She owed him the truth.

After driving into Truelove, he pulled into the driveway of the distinguished Breckenridge home. He couldn't help but remember the first time he came to this house to ask her grandfather's permission to date her.

He'd driven over in his family's old Chevy. Nervous as all get-out. Hands slick on the wheel. Totally intimidated. Yet compelled to come, even if Yates Breckenridge took one look at him and turned him away at the door.

When his eyes locked onto Kate's at their chance meeting in the meadow at the ranch, he'd known—*known*—that split second would change his life forever.

A moment of sudden clarity. At seventeen, it had appeared so simple to him. The rightness. The goodness of what they could be together.

Despite the fear of her grandfather's rejection, he couldn't not come. On pain of his life, he couldn't forget what he'd felt for her in that brief instant. Nor ignore the certainty he was made for her. As she was made for him. They were as inevitable as the rising of the sun each morning. Meant to be.

Bringing him out of past memories to the confusion of the present, Miss Martha Alice stepped out of the house onto the rounded brick porch.

As nervous as that first day, he ran his suddenly slick hands down the length of his Wranglers. Time and a hard-won maturity had since chipped away at his youthful surety.

Nothing was simple. Not with Kate. She—they—were complicated.

He got out of the truck and walked over to Kate's grandmother.

"Oh, my darlin' Jack." She embraced him. "It does my heart good to see you at this house again."

The older woman smelled just as he remembered. Like the flowers in her wonderful garden. Of roses and lavender.

It wasn't that they hadn't seen each other over the years. At church. In the café. Truelove was too small a place not to run into each other frequently.

But she was right. This was different. The first time since the funeral he and Martha Alice had truly talked.

Kate's grandmother pulled back to study his features. "I want you to know I've prayed for you so often… How I've prayed God would… That He would see fit to…" She blinked away the moisture that had gathered in her eyes.

He wasn't sure what she'd prayed for him. But he was grateful. When he returned to Truelove after finishing his enlistment, he'd returned broken and spent. He'd needed all the prayers he could get.

Jack kissed her soft, powdery cheek. "They must have

worked. When I came to the end of myself, I found God with His arms open wide."

"And a fine, strong man you've become in the Lord." The older woman's mouth trembled. He could see the effort it cost her. "If only my Kate could find the same peace, but I fear until she…" Martha Alice blinked rapidly. "Go around the house. You'll find her in her favorite spot in the garden."

He nodded and turned to go.

Kate's grandmother caught his arm. "Be gentle, Jack. Something's different about her. I can't put my finger on what it is. She won't talk to me, but there's an urgency about her. A determination to resolve things left undone."

Was Kate anxious to finally be rid of him because she'd met someone else?

The idea of Kate with someone—anyone—but him gutted him so that he could hardly draw an even breath. *Oh, dearest God. If that's true, help me to accept what cannot be changed.*

Stepping through the white picket gate, he entered Martha Alice's extraordinary garden. A haven of serenity. A refuge in a troubled world.

The early afternoon June air was scented with the aroma of old roses and herbs. Larkspur and foxglove swayed in the slight breeze.

Jack relished the warmth of the sun on his face and arms, but it was a warmth without the draining humidity of the North Carolina flatlands. One of the many reasons he loved the highlands of Truelove.

He spotted Kate deep in thought by the fountain. Due to the tinkling spray of the water, she didn't hear his approach until he was nearly upon her. He didn't want to startle her.

Judging from her expression, her thoughts weren't altogether happy. He took advantage of the moment to get his first good look at her. He drank in the sight of her like a man dying of thirst. Like the love-starved teenager he'd been once upon a time.

At five foot seven, she'd always been slender and willowy. But confirming his initial observation, he was sure she'd lost weight. Weight she couldn't afford to lose.

New creases carved her otherwise smooth brow. Lines fanned out from her eyes. Not laugh lines, though. Perhaps the result of a harsh African sun.

She looked sad. But more than that, completely and utterly alone. A self-imposed aloneness. Nonetheless, it broke his heart. Yet when it came to Kate and his feelings for her, not an emotion he could afford.

He cleared his throat.

She glanced across the lion-headed fountain. "Jack."

The sudden light in her eyes did dangerous things to his nerve endings. Weakening his determination to maintain his distance. To not remember who they were—*used to be*—to each other.

He folded his arms. "Can you explain to me how it is we're still married, Kate?"

At his harsh tone, she flinched. Despite her grandmother's entreaty for gentleness, he couldn't seem to help himself. It was either that or… His heart thundered.

He'd not come expecting this. But seeing her in this spot where they'd promised to love each other forever required a superhuman effort to not enfold her in his arms. To not smother her mouth with kisses. To not beg her to—

Jack drew himself up. He was a fool. When it came to her, a stupid glutton for punishment. "I signed and mailed the divorce papers." He winced, sounding far too much like CoraFaye.

"I know," she whispered. "I saw them on my attorney's desk in Virginia Beach two days ago. I went there first."

He dropped his arms, clenching his fists at his side. "I did everything you asked. What happened?"

She tilted her head. "I never received the documents to sign on my end."

"You're telling me the divorce paperwork was lost in the mail between Virginia Beach and Africa?"

Biting her lip, she nodded.

Out of self-preservation, he dropped his eyes from her mouth. The rosebud upper lip. The fullness of her bottom lip. Desperate for somewhere else to land his gaze, he settled for the space in the middle of her forehead.

He planted his hands on his hips. "How long have you known about this?"

"Only a handful of days." She tucked a tendril of hair behind her ear. His stomach clenched.

"My attorney's son tracked me down in Africa and called to let me know. His father had been in the midst of retiring. We were going to be one of his last cases. But he had a massive stroke. The son was in law school at the time. It was only after his father died and the estate was settled, he realized our case had fallen through the cracks."

Jack gritted his teeth. "Unfinished business."

She sighed. "Yes."

At the time, his lawyer had mentioned it was taking a long time to get the signed divorce papers from Kate. But struggling to start over again in Truelove, he hadn't followed up with his attorney. Reeling from grief and the shock of losing Kate, he'd willfully put the paperwork out of his mind. Some secret part of him half hoping Kate had changed her mind?

"So in your usual efficient way, you flew straight from

the heart of Africa to rectify the oversight. Thanks for the heads-up." He turned to exit the way he'd come. "I'll wait to hear from your new attorney." And meanwhile put in a long-delayed call to his own lawyer.

"I'm getting awfully sick of seeing your back, Jack Dolan," she growled. "That's not how we do things."

He spun around. "Just taking a page out of your play-book. Like how you turned your back on me when you disappeared in the Congo."

"I'm sorry, Jack. I can't tell you how sorry." Her shoulders slumped. "I'm tired. So very, very tired." She sank down onto the scrolled iron bench.

Jack stepped around the fountain. "Tell me what you want me to do. It's only a piece of paper, Kate."

Her head jerked. "It's not just a piece of paper."

Jack could see he'd shocked her. For the life of him he couldn't understand why. Hadn't her absence and her silence over the last three, impossible years been clear regarding her feelings about him and their marriage?

"Piece of paper or not, what real difference does it make? We were broken long before this. Are you with someone, Kate?" He tensed, bracing for the blow.

Her eyes widened. "Why? Do you care?"

Jack cared. Oh, how he cared. But he was only too aware he had no right to care.

"There's never—" Her voice wobbled. "The divorce wasn't the only reason that brought me stateside. There were other matters I needed to attend to." She looked away toward the crimson red poppies nodding in the perennial border. "I need to make my peace with the past."

"You came home for Liddy."

"I've had no home since Liddy…" She fluttered her hand. "Since you and I…"

He knew exactly what she meant. He might have returned to the ranch and the house where he'd grown up, but home had proved as elusive as the woman sitting in front of him.

"I'm not sure even now if I can do it." She raised her gaze. "I'm not sure I can face it." Her eyes bored into his.

The anguish in them almost felled him. And no matter how much she'd hurt him—how much they'd hurt each other—he could no more allow her to face this most terrible thing alone than he could will himself not to breathe.

Because once he'd loved her. His heart squeezed. Once?

His love for her had to be past tense. Her abandonment of him and their marriage… The years with no word from her. Only a fool loved someone who didn't love them back.

Jack wouldn't—couldn't—play the fool for Kate. Not again. And yet… Though she no longer loved him, he couldn't live with himself if he didn't do everything in his power to help her find wholeness. Or whatever it was she'd really come searching for.

The call to his lawyer could wait another few weeks. Perhaps by helping her, he could also help himself better accept the worst thing that ever happened to either of them.

Jack took a deep breath. "We'll face the anniversary together. You won't be alone through this, I promise you."

Her lips parted. "You'd do this for me? After everything—"

"*Because* of everything." He clenched his jaw. "Let's set aside our differences for Liddy's sake. For now at least, we can table this other business."

She cocked her head. "A temporary truce? A cessation of hostilities?"

Enemies. Or strangers. Was that what they'd become to each other? He didn't know which was worse.

Absorbing the hit, he jutted his jaw. "For Liddy's sake, the two of us who loved her the most will honor her memory on the anniversary of her death."

The death he'd caused. The marriage he blamed himself for destroying. The woman in the aftermath of which he'd wrecked.

She stared at him. A long, long moment. He held his breath, afraid to hope. As always, she held his heart in her hands.

"All right," she said at last. "Two weeks." She gave him a curious look. He used to be able to read her so well. "Let's only promise each other two weeks."

She held out her hand. He accepted it. Electricity zipped up his arm. She must've felt it, too.

Kate threw him a funny half smile. "Chemistry in spades." She squeezed his hand before letting go. "That was never our issue, was it?"

No, it never was. But he'd take whatever time he could get with her while he could. And finally wrap his mind around letting go of the love of his life forever.

Or at least relinquish the dream of her he'd kept in his mind all these years. He cut his eyes at her. Not sure the woman standing before him bore any resemblance to the golden Kate of his memory.

Perhaps for Martha Alice's sake, he could convince her to stay in Truelove. Yet with every beat of his heart, he already felt the clock ticking down the minutes. Two weeks to remind Kate who they used to be.

Who they could be yet again together?

Idiot. Fool me once... Jack took a step back.

With the ruthless compartmentalization born of his years in the military, he shut down the tiny seedlings of hope threatening to burst open the chambers of his heart. Reconciliation wasn't an option.

He turned on his heel.

"Wait," she called, an inexplicably wistful note in her voice. "Will I see you tomorrow?"

"Let me check my schedule." He threw the words over his shoulder. "I'll text you."

This time, *he* left *her*. Almost, but not quite running. Desperate with a sudden need for solitude. To lick his wounds. To shore up his barricades.

War had honed an already well-established sense of self-preservation. And despite the guilt he wrestled with, this same sense of self-preservation told him he couldn't trust her—shouldn't trust her—to not hurt him.

There'd have to be boundaries established. Shields put in place to protect a heart that was only just beginning to heal. A matter of emotional necessity.

Because if he let her get too close…when she inevitably left him—

This time he wouldn't survive.

Chapter Three

⟜ᤑ

Shaken after her encounter with Jack, Kate stumbled into the house. She found her grandmother in the kitchen. Gram took one look at her, and lips pursed, moved to the stove to put on the kettle. Martha Alice believed there wasn't much that couldn't be helped by a bracing cup of tea.

Her grandmother removed two small plates from an overhead cabinet. "I'll make you a sandwich. You look like you could use feeding."

The last thing she felt like was eating. But from the steely look in Gram's eyes, she knew better than to waste her breath. A few minutes later, they sat down in the breakfast nook.

She fiddled with the sandwich, tearing the bread into bite-sized pieces, which she pushed around on the plate. Her eyes fixed on the gold-edged rim of the delicate tea-cup, she was more successful in sipping one of her grand-mother's fruity summer teas.

"And here I believed you liked my chicken salad."

"I love your chicken salad, Gram." Her gaze snapped up. "I don't have much of an appetite today."

"Looks like you haven't had much appetite for some

time." Gram's mouth tightened. "You've lost weight since I last saw you."

After Liddy's funeral at the town cemetery, Kate hadn't returned to Truelove. There were too many memories here, mostly good ones. But the small mountain hamlet she'd called home also held far too many reminders of everything she'd once held dear.

She might not have been brave enough to face the remembrance of what she'd lost, but she spent a week with her grandmother elsewhere during work furloughs. They'd met two months ago in Atlanta.

Eager to change the subject, she took another sip. "Is this a new tea?" She savored the taste on her tongue. "Strawberry. It would make a great iced tea."

"Stick around for supper, and you can find out for yourself." Gram set her teacup into the saucer with a tiny clink. "What's this about you and Jack still being married?"

Kate squared her shoulders. "I imagined you'd be thrilled, considering how the first year I was in Africa your letters talked of nothing but how Jack and I should reconcile."

"I'm ecstatic to have you home." Her grandmother's brow arched. "But as I recall, you were adamant about filing for divorce, and none too happy with my views on trying to save your marriage."

Not one of her finest hours, she'd threatened to sever contact if Gram didn't stop talking about Jack. Her cheeks heated. One of many not-so-fine hours. Since Liddy died, her life felt like a series of train wrecks.

"What's changed? How is it you still find yourself married?"

Kate cast her gaze out the wall of windows overlooking the lush flower garden. "I only recently discovered there was a miscommunication with my lawyer stateside. The clinic was remote. The postal service unreliable."

Several beats of silence ticked by.

"Your lawyer could've talked to his lawyer. Still doesn't explain why you decided to come home."

She stole a glance at her grandmother. "I—I thought it was time to face the anniversary."

Gram sat back in the chair. "Is your intent to try to reconcile with Jack?"

"That's not possible." She touched her hand to her aching temple. "But I—I thought Jack deserved to know—"

"Quite the bombshell you dropped on him in front of practically the whole town." Her grandmother gave a ladylike sniff. "Knowing is perhaps the least of what you owe Jack."

She flushed. "He needed to know in case he... He..."

"In case he what, Kate?"

She pushed away the plate. "I mean so he could..."

Gram cocked her head, resembling a pert bluebird. "I don't think you know what you mean." Her grandmother's face softened. "You and Jack. Such a love story."

She shook her head. "Until it wasn't anymore."

Gram laid her palm on the tabletop. "It was the kind of love story people write songs about. A story for the ages."

"Like Romeo and Juliet? Heathcliff and Catherine?" She made a strangled sound in her throat. "Stories where everyone ended up dead or insane."

Although when she'd seen Jack this morning for the first time in three years... The feelings he evoked... Maybe *she* was going insane.

"What happened to Jack and me was probably as inevitable as what happened to Dad and Mom after I went into remission, Gram."

From the second they met, she and Jack had been like

bright meteors blazing across the sky. Only to burn out just as spectacularly. Unable to survive the fallout after Liddy's accident.

Her grandmother's wrinkled features became stricken. "What happened between your dad and Denise was complicated."

Instantly, Kate was contrite. As one grieving mother to another, she shouldn't have mentioned Dad. Reaching across the table, she took hold of her grandmother's hand. "I'm sorry."

Throughout the long ordeal of treatment, her parents had been Team Kate. But the cure had proved nearly as fatal as the disease. A grueling roller coaster of hope and despair.

When she'd finally achieved remission, their marriage was nothing more than a patch of barren soil. Where nothing, certainly not love, could grow. Less than a year after she was declared cancer free, her parents divorced.

Their decision completely blindsided the teenaged Kate. Almost immediately, her mother remarried and moved to Florida with her new husband. She and Kate were no longer close. And struggling under the mountain of hospital bills, her dad died prematurely at the age of forty in his sleep after a massive coronary.

Reeling, that was the summer she came to live in Truelove with Gram and Granddad. The summer she first laid eyes on Jack Dolan. And fell helplessly, hopelessly—irrevocably?—in love.

No. She and Jack were history. Done. A part of each other's past.

"You are not your parents." Her grandmother squeezed her hand. "I can still see the image of your face the day he proposed."

She yanked her hand free. "Please don't. There's no use revisiting a past that cannot be changed."

"I know what it is to lose a husband and a child. I loved your grandpa like I never loved another, but losing a child... Even a grown child like your dad was something altogether different." Gram's eyes became a blur of vivid blue. "It's an ache that never leaves you, but there is a way forward."

"Where was God when I got cancer, Gram? When Mom and Dad divorced?" Her chest heaved. "Where was He when Liddy fell, hit her head and drowned?"

"God was weeping alongside you, my dearest."

The sadness on her grandmother's face was almost more than she could bear.

"He was weeping right there beside you," Gram whispered. "Loving you all the while."

"Thanks, but no thanks." She lifted her chin. "That kind of love I can live without."

Her grandmother's forehead puckered. "Can you, though?"

Kate's breath caught. How did Gram know about— but, of course, she didn't. Her grandmother couldn't know anything.

She'd already spilled one secret today. Gram didn't need to know the other one. Not yet, anyway. And based on her worsening symptoms, Kate expected living wouldn't prove too long of a problem. "I just need to get through the anniversary, Gram."

After that, her plan was hazy. If she could, she'd spare her grandmother the pain she'd put her parents through. Something of her thoughts must've reflected on her face.

Gram's eyes narrowed. "What aren't you telling me, Katie Rose?"

Her face had always been too expressive, revealing far

too much of her feelings. "N-nothing." Kate got up from the table. "Let me help you with the dishes."

The rest of the afternoon she hoped she'd hear from Jack. She must have checked her phone a dozen times in case she'd missed a call or a text, but there was only silence.

Had he meant what he said about being there with her to face the next two weeks? She had only herself to blame if he'd changed his mind.

That night, she dreamed she was in Virginia again. In her waking hours, she managed more or less successfully to block out the images of what happened three years ago. But what her conscious mind chose to ignore, her subconscious could not.

It always began in the split second before life as she knew it ended. Jack pulling her aside and the brush of his lips against her neck. A murmured endearment. Her throaty laughter. The playful look in his eyes changing as he glanced over her shoulder. He'd thrust her aside. Leaping forward shouting Liddy's name.

She'd spun around. Horrible, horrible screams she only belatedly realized were coming out of her own mouth. She raced after Jack, the pavement hot on her bare feet. Fearing—somehow knowing—it was already too late. Jack diving into the pool only to emerge with their limp, ashen child in his—

Kate awoke, thrashing in the sheets, screaming for Liddy.

Her grandmother knocked on the closed door. "Kate, honey? Are you all right?"

As the sound of her cry echoed in the darkened bedroom, she clamped her hand over her mouth. A belated and futile gesture.

"Kate? Answer me, sweetheart. I'm going to come in—" The door swung open. Her grandmother stood outlined by the night-light in the hall.

She made a valiant attempt to pull herself together. "I'm okay. Just a dream." She brushed the curtain of her hair out of her face. "I'm sorry I woke you."

"At my age," Gram sat down on the edge of the bed, "sleep seems to be more of an optional activity than a necessity. Do you often have nightmares?"

"Not as much as in the beginning. But sometimes that feeling of helplessness to stop what I know is unfolding slips past my guard. I'm reliving the desperation. The sadness." She drew her knees to her chin. "Usually a sensation, a fleeting memory during the day, triggers the dream."

Gram took her hand. "The trigger possibly being seeing Jack for the first time in three years?"

She rested her cheek on her knee. "Probably. That's one of the reasons I left. No surprise, neither of us were coping well."

"I tried not to pry into the details." Gram bit her lip. "You were fighting?"

"No, it was the crushing silence that hung heavy between us. It was tearing us apart from the inside out. He wouldn't look at me. He could barely stand to be in the same room with me. I'd lost Liddy. I was so lonely. There were so many reminders of her. Of us as a family. I was afraid I was going crazy. I'm ashamed to admit, Gram, I took the coward's way out. I ran." She swallowed.

"You were hurting." Her grandmother smoothed a strand of hair out of her eyes. "You both still are. The longer you hold it in, my sweetheart, the worse it will get."

"Part of me died when Liddy died, Gram. I don't know

how to do a new normal. I don't know how to do a future without her in it."

Her grandmother's gaze took on the shadow of faraway memories. "A child is a part of his mother in a way no other human being can ever be."

Kate blinked furiously against her tears. "My last thoughts at night and my first upon awaking are wondering in those seconds when she fell and hit the water if she was scared, if she was cold, if she was in pain."

"Grief is a lifelong journey, my sweet. I wish I could tell you it wasn't so, but it is. Eventually, the good days will outweigh the bad ones."

"I'm not there yet, Gram. I'm not sure I'll ever be. It's like I'm stuck in a dark hole, and I don't know how to climb out."

"Losing a child is not something you ever 'get over.' You are forever changed, but there is life beyond loss, Kate. It can become a life of purpose, joy and grace again."

She swiped at the tears on her face. "Just when I think I've no more tears to cry…"

Gram patted her arm. "Never apologize for the tears. They water the soul, soothing the sting of its hurts."

She threw her grandmother a rueful smile. "I don't know what to do to feel better."

Gram looked at her a long moment. "It has been my experience it is better not to offer advice unless asked."

Fatigue—emotional and physical—lay like a heavy mantle across Kate's shoulders. If admitting she had a complicated, unresolved issue with her loss was the first step toward peace, perhaps asking for help might be the next step on the path.

She'd already lost everything that mattered. What did she have to lose but her pride in her own self-sufficiency?

And if she'd learned nothing else from Liddy's death, it was how utterly insufficient she was at coping with this—the worst thing that could ever happen to a mother.

Kate took a breath. "I'm asking, Gram. What helped you when Dad died?"

"The people in my life—family and friends in Truelove. Instead of running away this time, let them comfort you."

"You mean the same people who told me time will heal the hurt, or that Liddy's in a better place?" she huffed.

Her grandmother knotted her hands. "People feel helpless. They themselves struggle to face death. They're too often exasperating, but you must learn to forgive them. They cannot truly understand our grief because they're not members of the awful child-bereaved club we never asked to join. And the compassionate Kate I love would never wish on them that kind of knowledge, would you?"

"No," she whispered.

Her grandmother placed her arm around Kate. "I thought not."

She leaned into Gram. "So don't run away, and let Truelove love on me is your advice?"

"One more thing." Her grandmother's blue eyes watered behind her bifocals. "Stop dwelling on the worst day of your life with Liddy. Instead, concentrate on the other, sweet days you had with her. There were many."

Kate's mouth wobbled. "There were." And yet, not nearly enough.

"Liddy was so much more than that one day. It does her an injustice to only think of her death. Grief is not about forgetting her, but about finding ways to remember her."

She let the truth of Gram's words wash over her for a second. "How did I get so blessed to have you in my life?"

"When joy, not pain, becomes your first thought of

Liddy—" her grandmother gave her a tremulous smile "—you'll have your answer."

She hugged her. "I love you, Gram." The older woman felt more fragile than she recalled.

"I love you, too, sweetie pie." Leaning back, her grandmother touched her cheek. "It's past both our bedtimes. Tomorrow morning, more than just my 'do will be wilting. Glenda fitted me in for a shampoo and set at Hair Raisers first thing."

"Whew!" She made a show of wiping a hand across her brow. "Glad I don't have that on my conscience."

Her grandmother laughed. With a flutter of her fingers, she closed the door behind her. Leaving Kate alone in the dark with her thoughts.

Gram was right. Kate could choose what she wanted to remember. Lying on the pillow, she closed her eyes. Funny enough, the thing that popped into her mind was the silly game she and Liddy used to play.

In those days on the team in Virginia, Jack's schedule had been unpredictable. Operators had to be ready to fly off to some far-flung mission at a moment's notice. Which meant Kate had to be prepared, too.

Kate worked a long weekend shift so she could be available for Liddy during the week. She and the other team wives traded babysitting.

Still in her nurse scrubs, she would get home after Liddy was in bed. Because she loved watching her sleep, she'd sneak into Liddy's little bedroom. More often than not, Liddy would hear her coming, and those beautiful baby blues so like Jack's would flash open. After an exuberant hug, Liddy always wanted to play with the stethoscope hanging around Kate's neck.

"I want to wisten to your heart, Mommy," she'd say.

Kate would place the ear tips in Liddy's ears and position the bell on her own chest. "How does my heart sound, Liddy Mae?"

"It sounds real good, Mama."

"What's my heart saying, Liddy Mae?"

"Lubba-dubba. Lubba-dubba." The corners of her rosebud lips would upturn with an impish tilt. "You wisten to my heart next, Mommy." Liddy would press her forehead against Kate's. "How does my heart sound, Mommy?"

"It sounds real good, baby."

Liddy would laugh in delight. "What is my heart saying?"

Kate would purse her lips as if concentrating. "Lubba-dubba. Lubba-dubba."

"You know what lubba-dubba means, Mommy?"

Anticipating her daughter's response, Kate would smile. Always the same routine. Always the same reply. "What does it mean, baby?"

Liddy would throw her arms around Kate. "It means 'I lubba-dubba you, Mommy.'"

Falling onto the pillows, they'd laugh and cuddle... *Oh, my lovely, precious girl.*

"I love you, too, Liddy," she whispered into the darkness of the Truelove night. For once, instead of piercing sorrow, the recollection wrapped Kate in sweet comfort. And as she drifted to sleep, her last conscious thought was of that memory.

The soothing, steady heartbeat of her child.

Sleep eluded Jack as he tossed and turned on the bed at the farmhouse. As he'd done so many times in the years, he relived the day Liddy died over and over. Looking for a way—any way—he might have done something different and changed the outcome. Hoping the sheer act of repetition might at least bring numbness. But focusing on that day only served to flay open a wound that never healed.

Would never heal—losing his beloved daughter.

Just before dawn, he dragged himself out of bed. Owner and barn manager, he was usually up before 5:00 a.m. to feed and water the horses. But after a night of fitful sleep, he was behind schedule this morning.

As the first streaks of golden pink light peeked from behind Dolan Mountain, he threw on a pair of jeans, shrugged into a denim shirt and grabbed a pair of boots. Careful not to disturb his grandmother, he inched down the hallway toward the kitchen and eased out of the screened porch, closing the door behind him quietly. Perhaps he wasn't the only Dolan who'd found it difficult to sleep last night.

He sat down on the hard cement step and tugged on his boots. Dew glistened like diamond drops on the blades of grass in the lawn. The mad quest of his adrenaline addiction that propelled him into the top tier of America's elite military forces had died when he gave the doctor permission to turn off the machine keeping Liddy's body mechanically alive.

Jack turned his head toward the rapturous predawn burst of song from a wood thrush. He'd come to a place in his life where he needed only a horse to ride, the mountain before him and someone to share them with. He'd long ago come to grips with the fact that someone would never again be Kate.

Or thought he had until she returned to Truelove yesterday and upended his world with her unexpected announcement.

He scrubbed his face with his hand. They'd shared the most painful experience of their lives. But they'd also shared the most wonderful of experiences. "I'm not sure what to do to help her," he whispered into the gentle breeze ruffling the branches of the pecan trees book-ending the house.

As the sun climbed its way over the ridge, an idea took root in his heart. The beauty of a life, no matter long or short, should never be overshadowed by one terrible day. And just like that, he had a place to begin with Kate. Back to where as a family they'd begun. Here in Truelove.

He spent the next hour dispensing hay, grain and equine supplements to the horses in his care. After check-ing the water buckets, he crossed the barnyard to the house.

In the kitchen, his grandmother was dressed in her usual seen-better-days farm attire. Bacon sizzled in the frying pan on the stove. "Late start."

Jack poured himself a cup of coffee. "Didn't sleep much last night."

His grandmother harrumphed. "Don't need a rocket scientist to figure out where that blame lies."

Jack resisted the urge to roll his eyes. "Nothing to be gained in laying blame."

Not resisting the urge, his grandmother rolled her eyes. "I believe in calling a spade a spade." She pointed the long-handled fork at him. "I hope you gave Miss High and Mighty the what-for followed by the old heave-ho." She punctuated her words with a short, swift kick to the empty air with her garden clog.

"Look, Grandma…" He didn't want to get into this with her. "If you're going to spoil the morning with an ar-gument, I'll skip breakfast and head back to the horses." He grabbed for a piece of bacon cooling on a paper towel.

"Hold on there, mister." His grandmother slapped at his hand. "You're going to burn your fingers. Sit down. Nobody's missing breakfast on my watch."

Suppressing a sigh, he pulled out a chair at the scarred kitchen table and sat down. His grandmother meant well. It was either believe that or let CoraFaye drive him nuts. She took him to raise when he was eleven and to hear her tell it, he was still about that old.

"Bow your head." She set a plate of perfectly cooked eggs and crisp bacon in front of him. "Thank the Lord and eat your breakfast," she grunted. She slipped into the opposite chair.

He obliged and then dug into the food.

A tough old bird, she eyed him over the rim of her coffee mug. "You look right done in this morning." She chucked her long salt-and-pepper braid over her shoulder. It sailed over the back of her chair. "I worry about you with all you've got on your plate."

He hunched over the table. "Nothing I can't handle."

"What with running the ranch, you could put moving into your house on hold till next year."

The other ongoing bone of contention between them at the moment—he was building himself a house. Born of the wisdom of being married to CoraFaye for forty-aught years, his granddad had the foresight to leave a parcel of the ranch directly to him. Over the rest, his grandmother had a life tenancy.

He slathered his toast with strawberry jam. "We agreed it'd be better for both of us to have some space. I've got lumber being delivered this afternoon for the deck."

She motioned toward the screened porch. "For a view of the mountain, there's a perfectly good spot over here."

He took a bite of his toast. After chewing, he swallowed. "The house is less than a quarter of a mile across the meadow, Grandma. We'll see each other every day when I'm over here working the horses. You'll hardly know I'm gone, much less miss me leaving mud on your clean floors."

"You'll be missed." She set her mug onto the table with a thud. "Who'll make sure you have a clean shirt to wear? Who'll make sure you don't forget to eat?"

Guilt stabbed him. He'd done his best, but since his grandfather passed last year, Grandma had been lonely.

Maybe the overprotectiveness wasn't entirely her fault. He'd come to the ranch broken twice now. The first time after losing his parents. The second time, three years ago. Both times, she'd been the one to pick up the pieces. He owed her more than he could ever repay. Perhaps therein lay the trouble.

"I'll be fine. I am fine." He ran his hand over his head. "I need to get to work." He rose.

His grandmother got to her feet and picked up his empty plate. "You working near the corral today?"

Tensing, he reached for his hat hanging on the peg. "I thought I'd drop by town later this morning."

His grandmother whirled. "I can't bear to see you acting the fool over that woman. She's only got to crook her little finger and you come running like a whipped pup, looking for more of the same."

Mouth tightening, he settled the hat on his head. "While she's here, I'm going to spend time with her, Grandma. It's not your decision to make. It's my life and Kate's."

"Let's hope it's the final chapter of your life with Kate," she growled.

His gut twisted. "Probably so. But I'm going to do it and if you can't handle it?" He squared his jaw. "I can always spend the next two weeks bunking at Jonas's house."

As soon as the words—and the threat implied—left his mouth, he was ashamed of himself. His grandmother clutched the back of the chair, her knuckles whitening. But give or take a second, she rallied.

"Just you mind to keep that—that *woman* far and away from me. Otherwise, I won't be held responsible for giving her the tongue-lashing she deserves."

Seized by a sudden realization, he stared at his never-say-die, take-no-prisoners, pull-no-punches grandma. He chuckled.

His grandmother went rigid. "What's so funny?"

"You." He laughed. "I never saw it until now, but that's what's wrong between you and Kate."

She scowled at him. "And what exactly would that be?"

He swung open the door. "You're too near alike."

Behind him, his grandmother sputtered. Grinning, he beat a hasty retreat. Before she took a broom to him.

Chores to do first. And then—his heart jackhammered against his rib cage—he'd see Kate again.

Chapter Four

It took Jack a few hours to turn out the horses and clean the stalls. After his conversation with his grandmother, he struggled to hold on to the peace he felt in the early morning moments after dawn. Doubt ate away at him.

Was Grandma right about Kate? Was he setting himself up for further heartbreak?

As a SEAL, he was no stranger to hard work and sore muscles. But today he drove himself especially hard, finding an unexpected, though fleeting, respite from the pain that had dogged him since that ill-fated poolside picnic with the team and their families.

To avoid another argument with his grandmother, he phoned Kate while he was at the barn. Cell pressed to his ear, he waited for her to answer. A bundle of nerves, he paced the stable. Which was ridiculous. He and Kate had known each other since they were teenagers. They'd been married for over a decade.

She picked up on the second ring. "Hello?"

His heartbeat sped up. "Kate. It's me." He cleared his throat. "Jack."

"I know."

Her voice set his pulse galloping. "Could we meet this morning? To maybe catch up?"

"I'd like that. Where?"

His stomach did a treacherous, traitorous flip. He liked the idea of seeing her more than he ought to. She'd always had that effect on him. Old habits died hard.

"It's a beautiful day." He toed the floor with his boot. "Perhaps we could find a bench on the square and talk?"

"Sounds good."

What sounded good was hearing her voice after a long, three-year drought not of his making. Before he chickened out, he made arrangements to meet at the town square in half an hour. He made a quick pit stop at the farmhouse to retrieve a cardboard box he'd shoved into the farthest reaches of his closet. He also managed to dodge another encounter with his grandmother, pulling weeds in her vegetable garden.

Later at the square, despite his best efforts, his heart skipped a beat at the sight of her, waiting for him on the sidewalk across from the Mason Jar.

In a pair of cutoff faded denim jeans and pink flip-flops, she wore a cotton shirt in his favorite Kate color. The purple shade she called lilac. She must have worn a hat the entire time she was in Africa. Her complexion retained the creamy lushness of a rose.

Billowing around her shoulders, her hair hung loose and free. Fingers twitching, he shoved his hands into his pockets. Once he met Kate, he'd never so much as looked at another woman.

She watched the late morning breakfast crowd make their way in and out of the diner. Her wistful expression surprised him. She'd never cared for the simplicity of small-town Truelove, which he found so essential to his well-being.

He needn't kid himself. She'd never stay. If he had an ounce of sense, he'd hightail it as far away from her as he could. But time and time again, he'd proved how little sense had to do with his relationship with Kate.

So intent was her perusal of his cousin Maggie herding her brood into the Jar that he reached her side before she turned. "Kate…"

Her eyes went from something slightly less tortured to something he dared not contemplate. He inserted a deliberate space between them. Fences made for good neighbors. The same applied to boundaries with not-so-ex-wives.

Jack motioned toward the café. "Want to get coffee? Kara makes the best mocha lattes this side of the Atlantic."

"No thanks." Kate shook her head, momentarily losing him in the ripple of its silky, reddish-gold waves. "Too many people. Too pub—" She pinched her lips together.

Too public. Right. He whiplashed back to reality.

He'd always been a sucker for a wounded creature, but wounded creatures were often the most dangerous, lashing out at others in their pain. He must never forget this was the woman who'd walked away from him two weeks after they buried their child.

Jack's mouth hardened. "If you prefer, we could always meet at some dead-end logging road out in the national forest where no one can see us talk."

"That didn't come out the way I intended. I'm sorry." She touched his arm below where he'd rolled up the sleeves of his work shirt. The brush of her fingertips against his skin ignited an explosion in his chest. "I can't seem to say or do anything right since…"

Ashamed of his uncharacteristic outburst, he tamped down the surge of anger. She wasn't the only wounded creature in this mess they'd made of their lives. *Forgiveness, Lord.*

When he lacked the means to convey the deepest concerns of his heart, he'd taken to simple, but sincere, one-word pleas. God seemed to understand. And never failed to be there when Jack needed Him most.

"That was uncalled for. I'm sorry, too." He blew out a breath. "Can we start over again?"

Kate's eyes cut to his so quickly he startled. Her lips parted. A vein in the hollow of her beautiful throat above the collar of her shirt throbbed. And then he realized what he'd said. A turn of phrase? Or had something more honest slipped past his defenses?

Help, Lord. Being with her was awkward. Fraught with a universe of subtext. His heart appeared determined to betray his resolve at every turn.

She made a sweeping motion. "Why don't we sit over there on the park bench."

Behind the statue. Beyond the gaze of prying eyes. Out of sight. Out of mind. Despite his best efforts, when it came to her something that never worked for him.

Apparently, not a problem for her. Until a lawyer and a bleak anniversary brought him to her mind. Had she availed herself of what she'd believed to be her freedom? *Was* there someone else in her life? A colleague she worked with in Africa?

His stomach churning, a fierce flame of jealousy licked at his insides. "Sure." He clamped his jaw tight. "Lead the way."

They sat down. Both of them silent for a full minute. Neither, he guessed, knowing what to say.

"Do you ever wonder how everything that had been so right went so wrong?" She faced him, an earnest expression in her eyes.

Okay... Not going to beat around the bush. He could work with that. He even admired that.

Beating childhood cancer, losing her parents, a military wife earning multiple nursing degrees while he worked his way to earning a trident. Kate was nothing if not gutsy. Making her abandonment of him so unexpected. But Liddy's death had proved the one obstacle she couldn't fight her way past.

Somehow, his voice found its way around the boulder lodged in his throat. "I wonder all the time." He shot her a glance. "We certainly didn't lack passion."

"No." A mounting flush crept up her neck. "We didn't lack that."

As far as he could tell, they still didn't. Not judging from the soft look in her eyes. Or the palpable energy between them. The not-so-latent attraction he felt for her wasn't all one-sided.

"We might have done better to start off as friends." His voice went gruff. "Less all-consuming."

In the wake of their tragedy, their different ways of coping had ultimately devoured what they'd been to each other. What they'd been hadn't been enough to sustain them through such unimaginable grief.

Her brow creased. "You want us to be friends?"

"Why not?" He hunched his shoulders. "What have we got to lose?"

They'd already lost everything that ever meant anything to them.

A clash of emotions played across her features. "Do you trust me, Kate?"

Her gaze flitted to his. His heart thumped in his chest. The all-too-familiar specter of guilt crashed over him like a rogue wave, unexpected and deadly.

Jack dropped his head. "Although, after what happened with Liddy, I have no reason to expect you'd—"

"I trust you, Jack."

The warmth of her hand against his brought an unwelcome sting of moisture to his eyes. "If I'd been more alert, faster—"

"If-onlys will eat you alive." She squeezed his hand. "Trust *me* on that. So where do we begin?"

"We'll mark the anniversary of her death, but in the meantime let's celebrate Liddy by remembering her life with us." He planted his feet on the grassy lawn of the square. "I've had plenty of time to think, too. And I believe it's not so much a matter of how you die, but how you choose to live."

She tilted her head. "Gram expressed almost the same idea to me earlier."

He threw her a grin. "Great minds."

The corners of her lips lifted. "Still so full of it, Cowboy."

"As I recall, you used to love that about me."

Kate shifted away. "Jack…"

"Sorry." He held up his hand. "We agreed not to go there. I'll keep a tighter rein on my witty banter."

"Witty banter?" A teasing light danced in her hazel eyes. "Jack Dolan, ladies and gentlemen." She made a sweeping motion as if to an imaginary audience. "A legend in his own mind."

Jack laughed so hard tears leaked from his eyes.

How he'd missed this—her—them. But he had enough sense this time not to say that out loud. She was skittish enough as it was—skittish as a turkey in November.

Leaning back, he rested his arms against the top of the bench. "How would you feel about getting ice cream?"

"Right now?" She raised her eyebrow. "It's not even lunchtime."

"Liddy never met an ice cream cone she didn't like." Sitting forward, he cocked his head. "Nor her mother, either."

Kate's mouth quirked. "Ice cream cones never fall far from their tree?"

"Somethin' like that," he drawled.

He could tell she wanted to laugh. She didn't, but a light that hadn't been there before shone from her eyes. A mere ember compared with the vivacious Kate he recalled. Yet the glow of it was sufficient to warm him with a hope he hadn't experienced in three years.

Jack started to cup her cheek the way he used to, but at the last minute his nerve failed him, and he touched her arm instead. "It's going to be all right."

She swallowed. "Will it?" Her voice lay heavy with emotion.

"Yes." He wasn't sure how, but with God's help, it would be.

Kate pointed her plastic spoon at Jack. "I've never fully understood how a man who made his living off adrenaline-fueled missions in exotic hot spots around the world could claim that his favorite ice cream flavor was vanilla."

They sat at one of the white iron tables outside the ice cream parlor off the square. At this time of morning, they had the place to themselves.

"I'm a purist." He tongue-swiped the cone. "Call me old-fashioned—"

"Or boring."

He ignored her. "Creamy, delicious, refreshing goodness. Sweet and simple just like me."

She snorted.

He pointed his ice cream at her. "What *would* Miss Marth'Alice say about such unladylike behavior?"

Kate sniffed. "I say there's absolutely nothing wrong with coconut ice cream."

"Coconut *curry* ice cream." He shook his head. "Liddy would've said, 'dee-gusting.'"

Kate laughed. "I'd forgotten she used to say that."

"For someone as risk-adverse as yourself—" he cut a glance at her paper cup "—you select the weirdest flavors on the menu."

"One person's weird, Jack Dolan, is another person's—"

"Goat cheese infused with basil ice cream qualifies as everybody's version of weird ice cream, Kate."

"Okay… That wasn't the best choice I ever made."

Among a long line of poor choices. Her smile wobbled. Including walking away from Jack.

But refusing to allow her regrets to sour their time together, she changed the subject. "Favorite ice cream parlor? Go."

"Chincoteague Island Creamery."

She smiled. "My favorite, too."

Living in off-base housing in Virginia Beach, the Eastern Shore had been a favorite place to escape to when Jack had a weekend free. As easy as a short drive across the Chesapeake Bay Bridge Tunnel to the Delmarva Peninsula.

"And that quaint little inn in Kiptohanock where we…" She reddened.

His gaze bored into hers. "Where we spent several very enjoyable wedding anniversaries."

She put her hand to her throat. "Please don't…"

A vein pulsed in his jaw.

Getting up, he dumped his half-eaten cone in the trash receptacle. "We also stayed there when we took Liddy to the creamery. She loved the Coast Guard station duck race fundraiser, too."

"The inn was the owner's childhood home." Kate warmed to the memory of that special weekend. "She was so sweet. Liddy enjoyed playing with her children."

Sitting down again, he ran his hand over his head, lifting his hat and resettling it. "Honey and Sawyer still send us a Christmas card every year."

There hadn't been an "us" for a very long time.

She pushed the cup away. "You should go back one day."

His face clouded. "Not without you," he rasped.

Their gazes locked.

Something awakened inside her. And the tight fist of her heart unfurled. For a fraction of a second, she felt again what they'd once been to each other.

What they could still be?

Her breath caught in the back of her throat. That wasn't possible. *Was it, God?* Liddy was gone. And soon, so, too, would Kate.

Breaking eye contact, she rose, the chair scraping across the pavement with a screech of metal. Jack stood up.

With more than a trace of desperation, she grabbed her cup and headed for the trash can. This couldn't happen. She mustn't fall for Jack again.

Appetite gone, she threw the rest of her ice cream away. And realized she'd actually prayed for the first time since Liddy died. A small start, but a beginning nonetheless. What was it about this town?

Gram's greatest heart's desire was that Kate might yet find her way back to God. And Kate's greatest desire?

She just wanted home. Gram would say both desires were ultimately one and the same. Kate's shoulders slumped. She was tired of being sad and angry and bitter.

Home had always meant Jack. But she'd forever lost the right to ever be more than friends with him.

Fiddling with the brim of his hat, he joined her on the sidewalk. "Want to walk around the square before I head back to the ranch?"

No matter what her head told her, her heart leaped at the opportunity to spend a few more minutes with him. She was an idiot. Such an idiot.

She exhaled. "Give me the extended tour of Truelove."

"Won't take long. This is Truelove." Throwing her an easy grin, he led the way. "Not much has changed."

She sensed that wasn't true. She'd caught glimmers of new depths in Jack. Unsuspected deep waters, which would take a lifetime to explore. A lifetime she wasn't going to have.

They crossed the street over to the square. Strolling along the perimeter of the green, the scent of hay, leather and something uniquely Jack wafted across her nostrils. Setting her pulse aquiver. And her heart racing like a runaway horse.

"I expect you heard about the tornado that whipped through Truelove two years ago."

She darted a glance at the Mason Jar across the street. "Miss ErmaJean's great-grandson was born in the aftermath, right? Nearly on the floor of the café cooler where a group had fled for safety."

"Amber and Ethan's baby. They were a few years behind us in school. She's a nurse, too. Pediatric nurse."

Kate's nursing days were behind her. She'd never return to the clinic in Africa. She'd started to feel unwell the day before she left Africa. And from the instant her lawyer's son reached her on the satellite phone, that chapter of her life closed.

She'd miss the friends she'd made there. Miss the not-to-be-forgotten sunsets. But nothing compared to how she missed Liddy. Curled into her cot at night under the African stars. Tears misting her pillow.

They rounded the corner of the square. He continued to update her on people in Truelove they both used to know. She was content to listen to the sound of his voice.

She'd never stopped aching for Jack. Or at least, who they used to be together. Her gaze skimmed the pavement at their feet.

Another corner rounded. Someone over at the open bay of the fire station shouted a greeting. Jack threw up his hand, but they kept moving forward past the school and library.

"My cousin Zach. Volunteers at the firehouse. Owns the auto repair shop."

Between the Dolan side and CoraFaye's side, she figured Jack was related to half the town.

She moistened her bottom lip. "Zach still dreaming of Nascar pit crew glory?"

Jack grinned. "I see you remember him."

"Hard to forget the His-n-Her checkered flag hats he gave us as a wedding present." She rolled her eyes. "Zach is memorable all right. Like a lot of Truelove residents."

Outside Allen Hardware, GeorgeAnne placed terra cotta pots on the steel shelving of a sidewalk display. Kate was tempted to hustle him along before the matchmaker turned around and got the wrong im—

"Jack! Kate!" GeorgeAnne yelled from across the street.

Kate's stomach did a nosedive.

"Great to see you two enjoying the morning!" his great-aunt bellowed in case Florida and California hadn't heard her the first time.

Arms folded across her chest, GeorgeAnne smirked. Jack waved. She bit back a groan.

GeorgeAnne would have Gram on the phone in milliseconds. And once his grandma heard the news… Kate didn't mind for herself so much. But she hated for Jack to suffer the wrath of CoraFaye. She wouldn't wish that on anyone.

A funny sort of smile on his face, he stuck his hands in his pockets and whistled some happy, stupid, cowboy tune under his breath.

Taking his arm, she frog-marched him around the next corner. "Speaking of the tornado, were you here when it happened?"

"I was at the ranch with Grandma that afternoon. The horses seemed to know what was coming before we did. Eyes wild, they raced around the pasture. I've never seen the sky such a strange color. But in the unpredictable way of a twister, it leapfrogged over the ranch, spared us and Jonas's place next door but tore into Truelove something awful."

She shivered as they passed the town hall and police department on the other side of the street.

He drew her attention to the gaps in the line of majestic oaks that once ringed the square. "There's a campaign for families to sponsor the new trees planted in the empty spaces."

She knew far too much about empty spaces. "The new trees will never attain the stature of the old."

"Like humans, they just need time." He gave her a pointed look. "The old ones are reminders of the past. The new ones, a bridge to the future. Every time Parks and Rec puts another one in the ground, I'm filled with hope. For the town. For myself. That there is a way forward after devastation."

She came to an abrupt halt. "Time doesn't heal all wounds."

And they were back where they'd begun.

"No, it doesn't." His face gentled. "But it does blunt the rawest edges."

"I don't know how to move past what happened to Liddy." She choked off a sob. "To us."

"You don't have to figure it out alone, Kate."

She couldn't bear the intensity of his gaze. What he didn't know—couldn't know—was that time had run out for her. Alone was what she deserved.

"Jack…" She put her hand over her throat.

"Fine. Tell me about Africa." Blowing out a breath, he removed his hat and raked his fingers through his hair. "What was it like nursing there?"

"In the bush, a medical professional has to be able to do a bit of everything. It's all-consuming. Exhausting. Exactly what I wanted. No time to think beyond the current patient. No time to feel or remember."

"Or grieve? Maybe it would've been better for you if you had."

He wasn't wrong. "What you refuse to acknowledge in the daylight, you're forced to relive at night."

Jack's brow furrowed. "What?"

"Something Gram said." Determined to return the conversation to safer channels, she shuffled her flip-flops on the sidewalk. "What's it like being a full-time rancher?"

He steered her toward a bench. "Surprisingly good." He gave her that slow, easy smile, setting butterflies to dancing in her belly.

Careful, she warned herself even as she completely

disregarded her own advice. He was still so dangerously attractive. Dangerous to what little peace of mind she'd clawed out for herself in the shambles of her life.

"I've got friends. Family." He gestured at the blue-green horizon to the west of town. "The mountains."

Echoes of Gram's advice. What else might the old woman be right about? About her and Jack? About everything?

Foot bouncing on the grass, she jiggled her knee.

"Want to know the verse that helped me the most?" He looked at her with a hint of uncertainty. "Jack Dolan quoting Scripture. Kind of unbelievable coming from me, huh?"

It was hard to believe coming from her cowboy-SEAL. When they left Truelove, God hadn't been part of their lives. Her heart pricked. So much might have turned out differently if He had.

Jack rubbed the nape of his neck. "Only if you'd like to hear it, of course."

"I'd like to hear it," she rasped.

He cast his gaze toward the ridge. *"'I lift up my eyes to the mountains from where my help comes.'"*

"I can understand how you draw strength from this place."

They'd spent most weekends of their married life in nature, hiking, kayaking and other outdoor adventures.

"As far as it goes, there is a temporary truth in that." He shrugged. "It was only later I was able to appreciate the next verse."

"Which says?"

"Real, lasting help comes from the Lord, the Maker of heaven and earth. Help doesn't come from the creation but from the Creator. I'd spent my life looking in the wrong direction."

She looked at him for a long moment. "You've changed."

He dipped his chin. "Sorry."

"Don't apologize. I like this deep-thinking Jack Dolan."

Nearly as much as she'd loved the wild cowboy she'd married. Still loved?

"A newer, improved version." His rugged features broke into a lopsided grin. "I repeat, what's not to like?"

Shaking her head, she rose. "And on that note, ladies and gentlemen…"

He stood up, laughing. "Want a tour of the ranch? How about Monday? Come see what I've done with the old place."

"I'd like that."

Way too much as a matter of fact. If she had the sense God gave small animals, she'd run for those mountains he loved so much. Wait.

She'd already tried that, hadn't she? She'd headed for the hills of Africa. And look how much good that had done.

Time—and life—was short. No one was as much aware of that as Kate. She was here to say goodbye to those she loved. Did that include Jack?

Shying away from the implications of that, she found herself agreeing to come out to the ranch. Despite her better judgment.

Chapter Five

Jack walked Kate to her car, parked next to the curb. "I'm surprised you didn't walk over."

Not too long ago, she would have done just that. But she hadn't felt well this morning. She suspected she had a low-grade fever. And there was also the nagging headache she couldn't shake.

But no way in the world would she have turned down the chance to talk with Jack. And eat ice cream, too. She smiled.

He leaned against the car. "What's got you amused?"

"Thinking about coconut curry ice cream."

He made a face. She laughed.

"But I'm glad you drove." He hooked his thumbs in the loops of his jeans. "This will save me a trip to Miss Marth'Alice's. There's this box I've been meaning to give you."

"A box? What's in the—"

"Hang on." He double tapped the car roof with his palms. "It's in my truck. I'll be right back."

Jack jogged over to his GMC. He flung open the passenger side door and plucked something off the seat. Carrying a large, white cardboard carton in his arms, he hurried back to her.

"Very mysterious." She smiled. "What've you got in there?"

He looked hesitant.

"Jack?"

"When I didn't re-up and came home to help Grand-dad, I had to pack the contents of our apartment."

She sighed. "I'm sorry I left that for you to do."

"I also had to pack up Liddy's room."

Kate stilled.

Jack shifted the carton to the crook of his arm. "Most of the furniture is stored in Grandma's attic." He glanced down and then up again. "But the special stuff I thought you might like to keep. If you ever decided to return."

Her heart lurching, she took a step away from him. "I—I—"

"I think it would do you good to look through it. There're sweet memories in here. Don't lock yourself away from those, too." His Adam's apple bobbed in his throat. "Please."

"All right," she whispered. "I'll try."

"Good girl."

The smile he sent her winged itself into that special place in her heart that had always from the first moment belonged exclusively to him.

He handed her the box. "No pressure. No rush. What-ever time you choose."

Reality slammed into her. Time was fast running out. To make her peace with Liddy's death. With Jack. With God.

He helped her deposit the cumbersome box in the trunk of her car.

"Monday morning, the farrier's coming to shoe about

a half-dozen horses. He has the animals divided up so that every horse is either shod or trimmed on a six-week schedule. Once I get him sorted, I'll be free to show you around. Would ten o'clock work for you?"

"I'll look forward to that." And she meant it.

She stared after him as he drove away. An unexpected morning, but despite the often-hard conversation, a good morning. He wasn't the same Jack. In addition to the masculine cowboy swagger and his rugged good looks, there'd always been a sweet gentleness inside him. There was now maturity and wisdom, too.

His face lit up when he talked about the ranch. Truelove had been good for him. If she had more time, if she hadn't burned her bridges here—if horses could fly—it might have proved good for her as well.

She was about to get into her car when AnnaBeth came out of the bank and called hello. Leaving her vehicle, Kate walked the short distance to save the expectant mom a few steps.

The statuesque redhead gave her an exuberant hug. "I was so happy to finally meet you yesterday. I'm so glad you returned to Truelove."

Of a more reserved nature, Kate had never been one to go in for public displays of affection. Except with Liddy. As for Jack… She felt her cheeks burn. That side of their marriage had remained private but extremely affectionate.

"I know…" AnnaBeth fanned her face. "It's terrible."

Kate's heart nearly stopped. Had she expressed her thoughts out loud?

"Mid-June and already heating up." AnnaBeth laughed. "Although, maybe it's just me." She patted her belly. AnnaBeth's smile fell. "Oh. I'm sorry."

Someone had finally clued in AnnaBeth on Kate's

tragedy. And with Truelove being Team Jack—rightly so—it said a lot about the young woman that she'd made an effort to reach out to Kate again. But at least Anna-Beth hadn't guessed the true nature of her red cheeks.

"No need to be sorry." Taking hold of AnnaBeth's wrist, she felt for her pulse. "How are you feeling? Sorry." She let go of AnnaBeth. "Occupational hazard. Always trying to nurse."

AnnaBeth's green eyes sparkled. "You don't want to lose your skills." She chuckled. "Whatever that means. Amber's always saying that. She and Dr. Jernigan are the closest medical professionals Truelove had until you arrived."

Kate frowned. "I'm here temporarily. I'm not staying."

"I said the same thing when my car broke down in a snowstorm, and I met a cowboy of my own." AnnaBeth ran a light hand over her protruding belly. "Just look where I am now."

Gasping, AnnaBeth's eyes widened. "I've put my foot in it again, haven't I? Although, technically I hear you and your cowboy are still…still… I mean…"

Kate laughed. "No need to walk on eggshells." She motioned toward the Mason Jar. "Thanks to my big foot in my even bigger mouth, my current life ailments have become fodder for Truelove's gossip hotline."

AnnaBeth shook her head. "It wasn't that way at all. Miss IdaLee sat me down straight away so I'd understand and not make a mess of it. Yet here I've gone and done it anyway."

Sunlight gleaming through her Titian tresses, her hair was really most remarkable. As beautiful as the young woman was kind.

AnnaBeth fanned her face again. "So much for hoping we could be friends."

Kate used to have a lot of friends. Mostly, the wives from the close-knit SEAL community. Unsure how the just-friend thing would ultimately work out with Jack, she could use another friend about now.

"We can still be friends." She scanned the beads of sweat popping out on AnnaBeth's brow. "Are you sure you're feeling okay? How long have you been on your feet?"

AnnaBeth waved her hand. "Just running errands this morning, but I'm fine. Really."

"No offense, but you're looking a bit wilted."

AnnaBeth smiled. "None taken. Jonas's mom tells me if I think this is hard, wait for menopause."

Making a mental note to pack her nursing kit in the car next time, Kate wished she could've checked the mother-to-be's blood pressure. "Maybe we could grab a stool at the café. You should drink a tall, cool glass of water. I'd like to hear about your Christmas happily-ever-after with Jonas."

"I'd love to." AnnaBeth settled her purse on her arm. "But I'm due to pick up Hunter at the recreation center. Rain check?"

Feeling uneasy about the young woman, Kate insisted on escorting her to her car. AnnaBeth continued to extol the wonders of her stepson, a pint-sized lasso champion. It was abundantly clear how dearly she loved him.

"He'll be wanting lunch," AnnaBeth rattled on. "He's only eight, but Miss ErmaJean says by the time he hits his teens he'll be a ravening wolf, eating us out of house and home. Oh, no." She clapped a hand to her head.

Kate's heart skipped a beat. "What?"

"I forgot to stop by the grocery store."

Kate reminded herself to breathe. "Not cataclysmic."

"Didn't mean to scare you." AnnaBeth rolled her eyes.

"You don't even want to know how many gallons of milk we go through in a week." She stopped abruptly. "Sorry. Pregnancy fog brain. I used to be considered quite normal."

Kate laughed. Bubbly AnnaBeth was fun. Just what she needed more of in her life.

"Are you sure it's the baby?" She crossed her arms, pretending to be stern. "How long after you moved to Truelove did this madness begin?"

"It's a delightful madness." AnnaBeth clicked her key fob. The door locks opened. "But you're right. Truelove has a way of rubbing off on you. In the best possible way. Just what the doctor ordered. Good for what ails you."

Kate's eyebrow rose. "A dose of Truelove?"

The young mother batted her eyes. "Worked for me. Follow me to the center and I'll introduce you to Hunter. And Maggie. Oh, wait. I forget you're not a flatlander like me. You grew up in Truelove."

She shook her head. "I know Maggie, Jack's cousin, but I didn't grow up here. I only finished my senior year in Truelove. You don't get much more flatlander than this girl who called Vah Beach home for years."

AnnaBeth leaned heavily against the open car door.

Pinpricks of concern needled Kate. "When's your next prenatal visit, AnnaBeth?"

"Friends call me A-B." She shrugged. "I see my obstetrician every two weeks. Next month, we go to every week. Such a long trip. I don't ride as well as I used to." She put a hand to her back.

Kate didn't like the idea of her new friend heading up the serpentine mountain road to the FieldStone Dude Ranch. Maybe she would follow her, after all.

"On second thought, A-B, I'd love to meet Hunter. The

center wasn't built when I was here last. It's been even longer since I visited the FieldStone."

AnnaBeth's eyes shone. "What a wonderful idea. I'll text Jonas's mom to add an extra plate for lunch." Before Kate could protest, AnnaBeth folded into her dark blue SUV. "See you there."

She followed AnnaBeth to the center, but didn't go inside. A flotilla of half-day rec camp volunteers supervised the waiting children in a carpool line. Kate pulled into an empty parking slot well out of the fray.

Accompanied by a college-aged student armed with a clipboard, a young boy with chocolate brown eyes, the spitting image of his cowboy dad, Jonas, rushed over and got into AnnaBeth's car. A beach towel slung like a stethoscope around his neck, his hair was wet and slicked back. A hard knot the size of a peach pit formed in her stomach.

She hadn't realized the new center also contained a swimming pool. AnnaBeth's son had obviously just finished a lesson. It was that time of year. Nothing said summer like hot dogs, camp and swimming. Bile rose in her throat.

How many children would accidentally drown this summer? How many mothers would lose their babies to death by swimming pool? How many families would be torn apart by tragedy?

She reconsidered continuing on to the FieldStone. But her concern for AnnaBeth wouldn't allow her to shirk her duty.

When AnnaBeth pulled away, she put her car into gear and followed. Jonas's ranch was pretty much as she remembered. The main house, all wood, stone and glass, reminded her of a vintage national park lodge. The rustic cabins scattered across the landscape looked inviting.

AnnaBeth introduced Hunter to her. He gave her a shy smile.

"It's early in the dude ranch season, so only a few cabins are occupied right now. We're booked solid the rest of the summer. If you change your mind about staying in Truelove, you should come to one of the bonfires we do for the guests at the end of each week."

Kate had fond memories of roasting marshmallows here. During her courtship with Jack, there'd been more than a few stolen kisses at FieldStone bonfires.

Lunch with Jonas's mom, Deirdre, wasn't as awkward as she'd feared. The dude ranch was a family-run operation. Hunter wanted to show off his lasso skills. Kate was impressed. It was equally clear how much the little boy adored his stepmother, AnnaBeth.

"The seasonal wranglers arrive this weekend." AnnaBeth gave her a tour of the main lodge. "Just in time for our first full week of ranch activities. I usually oversee housekeeping, but this year Jonas and Miss Deirdre sidelined me." The pregnant woman sighed. "I'm better at staying busy."

Kate drew the line when AnnaBeth offered to take her down to the barn. "You spent the morning on your feet. A little rest would do you wonders." She smiled. "What they tell parents on airplanes is good advice for moms in general."

"Fog brain." AnnaBeth rubbed her forehead. "What do they tell moms?"

"You have to put on your own oxygen mask before you can help your children." Kate patted her shoulder. "Hunter and Baby Stone need their mom for the long haul. Don't neglect taking care of yourself. It's not selfish. It's good parenting."

Returning to Truelove, she passed the rec center again.

The idea of the swimming pool gnawed at the fringes of her mind.

Gram's eyebrows rose when she carried the white cardboard box into the house. "What's that?"

"Jack packed Liddy's special things for me." She set the box onto the fireplace hearth. "He thought it might be a comfort." But she backed away from it like it was a snake.

Gram laid aside the garden catalog. "He's probably right."

AnnaBeth wasn't the only one who needed a rest. The recurring headache sapped Kate's energy. At the moment, the only thing she wanted to do was close her eyes.

Gram got out of her armchair. "Aren't you going to look through it?"

"Later."

She was in no shape, physically or emotionally, to contend with those memories right now. She turned toward her bedroom.

"Where are you going?" her grandmother called after her. "Have you had lunch?"

Kate needed to lie down before she fell down. Because if she did fall, how would she explain that to her grandmother?

"I had lunch with AnnaBeth at the FieldStone." She inched farther toward the hall, desperate to make her escape. "Sorry I didn't let you know. I hope you didn't wait lunch on me. I have emails to answer. A few medical journals to look through."

Kate was aware she was babbling. As a teenager, something she'd done when she was hiding something from her grandparents. She hoped Gram wouldn't remember.

But Martha Alice Breckenridge never forgot anything.

"What's going on, Kate?" Gram's lips thinned. "What are you not telling me? Your face looks positively green. Did everything go okay with Jack this morning?"

A reckoning was coming about the return of her illness. But she couldn't face it now. *Please, God.* Not until after she dealt with Liddy's death. She just needed a few hours, a short nap, to replenish her strength.

She scrubbed her eyes with her knuckles. "Everything's fine with Jack. He's giving me a tour of the ranch Monday."

Not a lie. A diversionary tactic. As she prayed—she'd done more of that since arriving in Truelove than since Liddy died—Gram took the Jack bait.

The older woman's features transformed. "I'm so glad you and Jack are reconnecting."

Gram had never stopped praying she and Jack would get together again. With coherent speech fading given the pounding intensity of her headache, she left her grandmother to her illusions and stumbled into the bedroom.

Closing the door, she sagged against the panel. She'd thrown her grandmother a matrimonial bone to get Gram off the scent of her failing health. But give them an inch…

Gram probably already had her matchmaker cohorts on speed dial, planning the vow renewal ceremony.

She shouldn't have raised her grandmother's hopes. She and Jack weren't getting together again. She wasn't staying in Truelove. She was dying.

Falling across the bed, her last thought before exhaustion overtook her and sleep claimed her at last—*Help me, God. Please.*

At the church service the next day, it came as no real surprise to Jack when Martha Alice arrived alone, but he couldn't deny feeling disappointment at not seeing Kate there, too.

Monday morning as he shoveled hay into one of the feed bins, Jack heard the sound of tires on gravel outside the barn. He came out to find Kate parking beside his truck.

Despite a night filled with admonitions to guard his heart, the sight of her produced an uptick in his pulse. And a flood of bittersweet memories.

Like the moment the nurse laid their newborn child in Kate's arms. Or of Liddy propped on Kate's hip, while she chased Jack around her old car with a soapy sponge. Liddy had laughed and laughed at her parents' silly antics. And then there was another memory of how Kate had looked at him when she lay in his arms—

Stop it. He scoured his face with his hand. *She doesn't love you. Maybe she never did. Not the kind of love that lasts anyway.*

Those days were long over. Never to be reclaimed. *Get it through your thick skull, Dolan. Don't wreck the day before it's begun.*

He and Kate were friends, or hopefully on their way there. And friendship was far better than the nothing he'd existed on without her these last three years.

Lifting his hand, he called to her. Answering his wave, she headed over to him. Her proximity restarted the thundering drumbeat of his heart.

Friends, Lord. Friends.

She'd come dressed for the ranch in fitted jeans, but she appeared tired, as if she hadn't rested well. No matter what she wore, though, she always looked good to him. The flattering curve of the short-sleeved turquoise top set his pulse pounding.

"Mornin', beautiful," he drawled.

It surprised him how even his tone sounded. Nonchalant. Mr. Cool. As if his entire existence didn't rise and fall with the crumbs she threw his way. A smile. The touch of her hand. A glance.

Pathetic, Dolan. Simply pathetic. *Get out of my head, Grandma.*

A becoming blush bloomed in her cheeks. "Morning yourself, Cowboy."

"Ready for the tour?"

He was absolutely rocking the calm, cool, collected vibe. A smokescreen for the absolutely knee-knocking jangle of nerves being with her inspired.

She smiled. "I've been looking forward to this."

He'd spent the better part of the last twenty-four hours looking forward to seeing her.

Squaring his shoulders, he steered her toward one of the barns. "Let's start in here."

He gave her a quick overview of the outbuildings.

"Wow. You've got quite the operation going here."

So far, so good. Keep it light. Stick with what you know.

"I didn't know how much the ranch had fallen into disrepair nor about Granddad's growing infirmity until I came back." He stopped to check on the farrier and then they went into the indoor arena. "We've got about five hundred acres, but that includes the mountain, too."

She threw him a smile. "Perfect for trail rides."

"We offer full, partial or self-boarding. Horses are expensive to keep. If everything goes as planned, by summer's end the ranch should be in the black again."

Hands on her hips, she did a slow three-sixty surveying the arena occupied by a rider under the direction of a trainer, guiding an appaloosa through a series of precise circles and stops while in a canter. "You've made so many improvements."

"I have a part-time trainer and several barn assistants to help me care for twenty horses. We're a bare-bones operation right now. Successful stables specialize these days."

They moved outside toward a corral.

He leaned his arms against the railing. "Grandad's dream and mine was to create an equestrian center here. We make our money on boarding. We'll make the Dolan Ranch name by training riders and winning shows."

She cocked her head. "Somehow I'm not picturing you in a jacket and jodhpurs."

He threw her a look. "We specialize in Western style. Rodeo. Barrel racing. Reining. Horsemanship."

She smirked.

He nudged her with his elbow. "But I know you knew that about me and the Dolan Ranch. Summer camp begins next week. With school out, I'll have plenty of riders eager to barter chores for reduced boarding rates."

"Tell me about what boarding involves."

He pushed the brim of his hat an inch higher. "Why? You thinking of boarding a horse with us?"

She tossed her hair over her shoulder. "I might surprise you."

"You've already got a horse boarding with us." He gave a sharp whistle, and a beautiful chestnut mare trotted over from the rest of the herd to the fence. The horse nickered and nudged her head at Kate.

"Oh, Jack!" Kate's eyes shone. "You've kept her. She's still here."

A surge of pleasure shot through him at her pleasure. "Of course she's still here. Fancy was your wedding gift from Granddad. She belongs to you."

Murmuring endearments, Kate rubbed Fancy's nose. "I can't believe she remembers me."

"Horses have long-term memories of the bond they share with special humans in their lives, even after a period of separation."

As a teenager, Kate had taken to riding like a duck to water. They'd shared so many special times together riding the trails around the ranch together.

"Fancy would love for you to take her for a ride this week."

As if the sun had become momentarily obscured by a cloud, a shadow fell over Kate's face. "I'd love that, too." She glanced away and back at him. "If I'm able, I will."

Jack's stomach knotted with a strange foreboding.

Chapter Six

Unsure what she meant, Jack frowned at Kate.

"I want to see everything." Throwing off whatever melancholy she'd fallen into, she became brisk. "You were going to tell me about your boarding services."

"Blanketing, grooming, riding or training services. In addition to full access to our arenas, trails, tack room and wash stalls." He walked her around the facility. "Daily turnout to pasture. We have five. Each fenced pasture has an automatic watering system. Mares and geldings are pastured separately."

Kate's eyebrows rose. "Automatic watering and fencing sounds expensive."

"Don't get me started on the astronomical cost of hay. When I took over, everything needed modernizing. A veterinarian is on call twenty-four/seven." He stopped beside one of the pastures. "I think you may have seen her in town the other day."

"The blonde?"

"Uh… Yeah. Ingrid." At the strange note in her voice, he crossed his arms. "Why?"

Kate's perfectly beautiful lips pursed. "Ingrid."

Having long ago decided women were a mystery best

enjoyed but left unsolved, he moved into the stable. He paused beside a stall occupied by a large bay horse who thrust its head out of the stall opening. "Meet Carrots."

Stroking its velvety nose, Kate smiled.

"We offer foaling and recovery services, too. Carrots is recovering from an unfortunate encounter with barbed wire."

"Oh, no."

"An injury he sustained before the owner had him moved into our care." Jack moved down the row of stalls. "Let me show you the lounge, finished in time for our summer campers. There's drink and snack machines, a microwave and refrigerator."

She followed him, reading the name posted outside each stall. "Fuzzy. Guacamole. Doodle. Cupcake. Skidaddle. Wasn't that what Liddy wanted to call her—" She halted midstep. "You don't mean to tell me you still have Liddy's pony?"

They'd gone to the Chincoteague Fire Department's world-famous pony penning weekend on the Eastern Shore for Liddy's birthday. Jack's grandparents arrived for the auction with a horse trailer in tow.

"Liddy loved horses."

Kate tilted her head. "Like her father."

He squared his shoulders. "And his father and his father before him."

A gift from Jack's granddad to his great-granddaughter. Liddy picked out the foal she wanted, and Granddad bid on him. Two weeks later, she drowned.

"She never got to ride h-him." Kate's voice cracked.

Jack looked at his boots. "Later, it gave Granddad a great deal of comfort to train her pony. Skidaddle gives beginner riders a lot of joy." He rubbed his chin. "Would you like to see him?"

Biting her lip, she nodded.

Leaving the barn, he steered her toward one of the paddocks. "I took over his training after Granddad passed." He motioned toward the black-and-white pony munching on grass. "Twelve hands. He seems to have a special affinity for children. He's very gentle around them."

She toyed with the silver hoop of her earring. "Liddy chose him because his blue eyes were like her and her daddy's."

Jack smiled. "Skidaddle loves the games we do with the lesson kiddos. He's happy to follow along." He smirked. "Although if allowed, he can be bossy, even with the bigger horses. Gutsy and confident in the pasture and on the trail."

She shot him a look. "Not entirely unlike our daughter."

Traits Liddy inherited from both her parents. His smile dimmed. A little more fear might have kept Liddy away from the pool and saved her life. But what had happened couldn't be undone.

Diverting the conversation away from dark waters, he gave Kate a rundown on his daily routine at the ranch. "Lessons with riders continue all day until the barn closes. Morning riders tend to be moms who've dropped off their kids at school, retirees or people on vacation."

Leaning against the fence rail, she watched Skidaddle trot around the paddock.

"During the school year by three p.m., we're in full-swing lesson mode as the kids get out of class and head to the stables. I teach those classes myself."

She looked at him. "You like working with the children?"

"I do." He gave her a sheepish grin. "Big surprise, huh?"

"Not to me." She patted his arm. "You were always good with Liddy."

"When I was home, you mean?" He kicked the post with the toe of his boot. "The ops took me away so much. I regret that now."

"It was your job. It was your life."

As he gripped the top rail, his eyes latched onto Skidaddle. "You and Liddy were my life. Too late, I realized that. I'm sorry, Kate, for how often I left you to do everything alone."

"You've changed." She turned toward the paddock, her shoulder resting against his. "In a good way. Better."

At the feel of her skin through his shirtsleeve, he closed his eyes for a second. He savored her nearness, something he'd never dreamed of knowing again. They might only have this week to help each other heal, but he was grateful for the chance to be with her one last time.

He sighed. "About time I grew up, I reckon."

"Me, too." She nudged him. "What happens after the lessons?"

He swallowed. They'd been close to venturing once more into treacherous undercurrents best avoided. "Five o'clock, the horses come in for evening feeding and water check. The staff leaves. The barn closes by eight. I do a bed check at ten to make sure all's well with the horses and that the stable is battened down for the night."

She stepped away from the fence. He immediately felt the loss of her warmth.

"That's a long day."

"Not to mention the all-nighters I may have to pull for a sick or injured horse. And there's always maintenance to be done on the facility or pastures."

She gave him a quick smile. "Never a dull moment. Exactly how you like it."

Lifting his hat, he settled it down again on his head. "You know me too well."

"Your granddad would be so proud of the direction you've taken the ranch."

"I never envisioned myself back here." He scanned the mountain beyond the pastureland. "Never imagined a future apart from the team. But when Liddy... And you..." He took a breath. "Granddad got sick, and Grandma needed me."

A silence fraught with so many emotions arose between them.

She twined her fingers through his. Shocking him. "But it suits you. I've never seen you so..."

"*Content* is the word I think you're searching for." He glanced at their interlocked hands. "And peace from knowing I'm right where I ought to be."

As for happiness? Not since Kate and Liddy left his life.

"I envy you that," she whispered. "If I could only discover how to get what you've found."

"No big secret. God, family and Truelove."

She disentangled her fingers from his. "In that order?"

He heard the skepticism in her voice. An old adage yet true, he could lead a horse to water, but...

Much as it pained him, he didn't push. Grief was a devastating journey. The path unique to each person. There were signposts along the trail, but ultimately she would have to choose her own way home. He only wished she understood she didn't have to make the journey so completely alone.

"How would you feel about doing some work today?"

"If cleaning out the stalls is the price for a ride?" She smiled. "I'm game."

"Nothing so strenuous." He gave her a critical look. "A stiff wind might blow you away."

She flexed her bicep. "I'm stronger than I look."

"Of that I have no doubt." He folded his arms. "You're the strongest woman I've ever met."

"I wish that was true."

"You don't give yourself enough credit. Getting up every morning is sometimes the bravest thing any of us can do. And I speak from experience."

A tender look softened her eyes. "It helps to know you get that. What else do you have in mind this morning?"

"Blueberries are ripe on the lower slope." He cut his eyes at her. "If we pick 'em, you think Miss Marth'Alice would make me one of her award-winning cobblers?"

"I think something could be arranged." Her mouth quirked. "She likes cowboys."

Sticking his thumbs in the corners of his pockets, he leaned against the rail. "What's not to like, darlin'?"

"Give me strength…" She pushed at his shoulder. "But it's good to know some things never change. Like that massive ego of yours."

Laughing, he straightened. "Morning picking gets the sweetest berries. Let's get those buckets. Afterward, we'll grab lunch at my house."

"Hold on there, Cowboy." She ground to a halt. "Is this going to involve CoraFaye? No offense."

"None taken. And no, it does not." As easily as if he'd done it just yesterday, he slipped an arm around her shoulders. "Lunch at my house. Prepare to be amazed at the extent of my adulting these days."

"You have a house?"

"Try not to look so shocked. We talked about getting a house before…" He grimaced.

For him and Kate, time would always be divided into Before and After Liddy's death.

"You never cease to amaze me." She gestured. "Look at what you've accomplished. I'm so proud for you."

Already he beheld a difference in the brittle, bitter Kate who'd shown up in his stable yard three days ago and the woman standing before him now.

Being home was good for her. Being with the people who loved her was making a difference. Being with him...

Could it be true, Lord? Are you doing something here for Kate? For us?

His heart swelled with hope he could convince her to stay. Not for him, but for herself. *Yeah, right. Tell yourself another one, dude.*

Gazing over the distant purple-blue ridge, she took a deep lungful of air. "I've always loved this place."

I always loved you. His heart jolted painfully. And whatever tight rein he was trying to keep on his heart slackened.

He'd never loved another woman like he'd loved Kate. He suspected he never would. But there were no clouds on the horizon today. And he gave himself up to enjoying the pleasure of her company. No second-guessing himself.

Jack gave her a slow smile. "Let's pick some blueberries."

They rode in his truck to an open clearing where immense bushes of blueberries grew wild. He handed her a tin bucket, similar to the one he carried. Using his thumb, he gently rolled the berry off the stem and into his palm. "It's not ripe if you have to tug, or if they're still pinkish."

"Got it." She pushed back her shoulders. "I'll probably have this bucket filled before you do."

He leaned back, arms folded across his chest, in a wide-legged stance. "You think so?"

She tossed her hair over her shoulder. "I know so, because I pick more blueberries than I eat, Cowboy."

Hands on his hips, he broadened his shoulders. "We'll see about that."

Over the next thirty minutes on either side of the mass of bushes, they picked their way down the row. The plink of blueberries hitting the bottom of the bucket was gradually replaced by soft thuds as the buckets filled with the ripe fruit.

He trash-talked her berry-picking skills, hoping to throw her off her game. She gave as good as she got. He'd surge ahead a few feet only for her to overtake him.

"Should've known not to throw down the gauntlet with someone as challenge-driven as a SEAL," she grumbled at one point, although good-naturedly.

"I'm not the only super-competitive blueberry picker out here today."

When she didn't answer, he crept around the bush to find her stuffing her mouth with a handful of berries.

"Caught in the act!"

Berries sputtering, she screamed and threw a handful from the bucket at him before taking to her heels and running.

"You better run, darlin'," he yelled and gave chase.

Laughing, they ran around pelting each other with blueberries. Finally, cornered against a bush with all avenues of escape blocked, she raised her hand, palm out. "Stop."

Armed with blueberry ammunition, he lifted his arm. "Do you concede my superior berry-picking skills?"

Swaying, she put a hand to her head. She went pale.

He dropped the blueberries and took hold of her arm to steady her. "Are you all right?"

"The elevation. Not used to running…" She sucked in a breath.

He gripped her arm. "Are you sure you're okay?"

"I'm fine. Really." She looked at their path strewn with blueberries. "What a waste."

"A gift for the birds. We've got enough for Grandma's jam and Miss Marth'Alice's cobbler."

He guided her to the truck. He took their buckets and placed them in the truck bed. "Sit down for a few minutes and catch your breath." He lowered the tailgate and helped her clamber up.

After removing a water bottle from a red cooler, he handed it to her.

"Thanks," she said.

When he leaped up to sit beside her, the truck rocked. "Don't want you getting dehydrated."

She surveyed the brimming buckets. "CoraFaye won't be pleased you picked them with me."

"Probably not. But it won't be the first nor the last time I disappoint her."

Tipping his head back, he guzzled the water. When he caught her staring, she blushed and looked away.

"Remember when we brought Liddy here?" Kate curled a strand of red-gold hair around her finger. "Gram read that book to her—*Blueberries for Sal*."

He chuckled. "And she spent the majority of the morning looking for the bear."

She smiled. "When she wasn't stuffing her face with blueberries."

He sobered. "Are you doing okay in Truelove, Kate? With me? Back where we began?"

"It's not as bad as I feared." She unscrewed the cap

on her bottle. "It's nice to be able to talk about her with people who loved her." She looked at him. "Sharing the memories with you. This is the happiest I've felt in a long time."

Something eased in his heart. Her words were a gift. "I've tried to think of her death less and think more about her life. It helps."

"But can I be happy when she's not here to be happy with me?" She gave him a crooked smile. "How messed up is that, huh?"

"I think it's okay to be happy again, Kate. It's okay to laugh. Liddy would want us to be happy. And I believe where she is, she's happy and she laughs often."

She scanned his face. "How can you know for sure, though? How can any of us?"

"We can know few things beyond a shadow of a doubt. But God made promises to His children. And I've made a choice to trust Him." He blew out a breath. "I don't think it's a betrayal of Liddy to choose to be happy again. Choosing to live life fully is a tribute to her. To laugh, especially about a memory we created together, is the best kind of legacy. A lasting legacy to all she was."

Kate closed her eyes. The breeze played havoc with her hair. He fought the urge to take her into his arms. Longing to kiss the hurt away, if at least temporarily. She'd made it clear she didn't need or want him.

Every time he was with her, the walls of his self-imposed protection crumbled a little more. She needed a friend more than she needed a husband or a lover. She was seeking something—someone—like he'd never known her to search before.

Finding that was more important than anything they might share. He refused to do anything to upset the careful, high-wire balancing act she walked toward home. Her truest home.

But sitting this close to her, the heady scent of her honeysuckle lotion teased his senses. Not a torture he could withstand for too long without losing the battle within himself. Inching to the edge, he jumped off the tailgate. Landing on his feet, he planted his boots firmly on the ground of their current reality.

He stuck his hands in his pockets. "We should probably think about what we want to do next week for the anniversary."

"Sounds like you have an idea."

He shrugged. "Just an idea."

"Go ahead." She jutted her chin. "I'm listening."

"Miss Marth'Alice and her committee are raising money to plant trees on the square to replace the ones lost." He scuffed the toe of his boot in the dirt. "Thought it might be nice to dedicate one to Liddy's memory. Get a plaque with her name on it. Have a tree-planting ceremony. Liddy's tree would give rest and shade long after you and I are gone."

She didn't say anything.

His gut twisted. "'Course, if you'd rather not—"

"I like the idea. A tree is a thing of beauty." She tucked a tendril of hair behind her ear. "Just like Liddy."

Just like her mom.

His heart pounded. "I should get back. The vet's coming to check on one of the mares after lunch."

A cloud passed over her features. "Ingrid?"

"Dr. Abernathy. She's great."

Kate's lip curled. "Is she, Jack?"

He pinched the bridge of his nose. "If you have something to say, spit it out, Kate."

"All right." Her eyes turned stormy. "Are you in a relationship with the vet, Jack?"

"What?" He reeled. "No. Where did you get that idea?"

"That first day…" Her gaze seared him. "I saw you outside the diner."

For a split second, anger surged, hot and tight in his chest. Followed by bewilderment and a growing realization whatever might have sprung between him and Ingrid had died an irreversible death the day Kate returned.

Why did everything always come back to Kate for him?

"I'm not going to lie to you. Ingrid and I have been friends for a while now." Taking off his hat, he stabbed his fingers through his hair. "We have a lot in common. We both love horses. I was meeting her for lunch the day you saw her. We were going to talk about taking our friendship to the next level."

She bit her lip. "I had absolutely no right to ask you that. Not after the way I—"

"Is there someone in your life, Kate? Is that why you really came back to Truelove once you learned we were still married?"

Her eyes swept over him. "There's never been anyone but you."

Jack's heart slammed into his breastbone. The moment stretched taut between them. An eternity of things that needed speaking yet remained unsaid.

Then she looked away. "You said you needed to go." She scooted forward.

He reached for her. "Let me help."

She slid down between his arms. Two fingers under her chin, he lifted her face, bringing her eyes level with his.

As his fingers trailed across her jawline, he loved the

soft smoothness of her skin. The impulse to kiss her wreaked havoc with his friends-only resolve.

Fortunately, his good sense prevailed. Brushing her shoulder, he let his hand drop. He pushed his hat lower over his eyes. For the sake of his heart, he carefully inserted some distance between them.

All the way back, Jack kept a tight grip on the wheel and his emotions. The truck jostled along the bumpy dirt path over the grassy hillocks. Silent beside him, Kate kept the buckets of berries positioned between her feet, preventing them from tipping over.

She broke the silence when he turned down the lane to his house. "Where are you going?"

"I promised you a house tour."

"But your…your—" Her mouth flattened. "Your vet is coming over."

He pulled the truck to a stop under the shade of a pecan tree. "A man's got to eat. And you look like you don't need to skip a meal." He thrust open the door. She didn't move.

"I'm hungry. And tired. And—" He tugged at the back of his neck. *Lonely.*

Throwing open the door, she got out. "What about the blueberries?"

He rested his arms across the frame of the door. "After lunch, I'll drive you to your car."

"I can walk."

"Stop being so stubborn." He pushed off the truck. "I've got to go that direction anyway. You can take Miss Marth'Alice a bucket, and I'll give Grandma hers. Help me put together the sandwiches. Please."

Her mouth set in a thoroughly unpleasant line, she glowered at him. "Fine. If it's that important to you. Since you said please."

Jack threw her his most charming, surefire, guaranteed-to-soothe smile. "Fantastic."

She rounded the hood. "Marvelous."

"Outstanding."

She marched ahead, not waiting for him. "Whatever."

"Hold on there, Nurse Cranky." He caught her sleeve. "I parked where you'd get your first, best view of my work in progress."

She laughed in spite of herself.

As he gave her the grand tour, she made appropriate admiring remarks. He was especially gratified when she gave an excited exclamation and plopped down in the window seat he'd built overlooking the mountain in the master bedroom.

He ended up making their sandwiches. She was too busy running her hand over the clean, sleek feel of the white quartz countertop in the kitchen. They sat at the stools lining the island.

"It's beautiful, Jack."

He took a bite, chewed and swallowed. "Lifelong dream of mine to build a house."

She craned her neck, taking in the wide-open space of the kitchen and living area. "How much more do you have left to do?"

He assessed the living space as if seeing it through her eyes. "Not much. I'm down to punch list items."

She wiped her fingers on a napkin. "When will you move in?"

"When it feels like it's time." He smiled. "You're my first guest."

She put her hand to her chest. "I can't believe you've done all this yourself."

"I've worked on it as I had money for materials. A labor of love. Just needs furniture and a woman's touch."

Smile faltering, she slipped off the stool. "I should go."

"There's no rush." He rose, too. "We still have time."

"No, Jack." Her voice took on an inexplicable sadness. "We don't. And besides," She cast another look around the spacious room. "I don't want to get in Dr. Abernathy's way."

It didn't take long to put the kitchen to rights. During the short drive through the trees to the main stable and farmhouse, something different hung in the air between them. She'd grown quiet. Too quiet.

Something had shifted between them. And he was desperate for another opportunity—any excuse—to see her again.

In a swirl of dust, he parked beside her car. "How about the trail ride we discussed to get reacquainted with your horse, Fancy? Tomorrow?"

"What am I doing here?" She stared at the ceiling of the truck cab. "What are we *doing*, Jack?"

His heart constricted. "You said it yourself. The time is short. Why not, Kate? Why not?"

A bleak expression flitted across her features. Gone so quickly he wasn't sure he hadn't imagined it.

"I never could say no to you." She heaved a sigh. "Tomorrow."

Shoving open the door, she threw herself out of the truck. Her hand wrapped around the handle of the blueberry bucket, she got into her car. His chest aching, he watched her drive away. *What am I doing?* Just as well she hadn't said goodbye.

It was becoming increasingly hard to imagine ever saying goodbye to her again.

Chapter Seven

Kate left Jack just in the nick of time.

Headed toward the road, she passed the coolly blonde and beautiful Ingrid Abernathy in her sleek front-wheel drive on her way toward the barn. Toward Jack.

Strangling the wheel, Kate descended the winding road toward town. Confusion warred with a strange sense of elation. The towering peaks of the tree-studded Blue Ridge flashed by on either side of her car.

In the pricey Tidewater Virginia real estate market, they'd been saving for a down payment on a home when Liddy died. They'd spent years dreaming about the modern-farmhouse vibe Kate adored. She'd been floored—speechless—as Jack proudly showed her around his house. The longer she sat in his new home, the more she envisioned herself there. In every room. Like she belonged.

The house—Jack's house—was everything they'd once talked about wanting in their forever home.

He'd built that house for her. *No.* Surely not. She was being ridiculous. Imagining something that wasn't there.

And yet... The evidence had been before her eyes.

The classic white exterior with black-framed windows.

The pop of color on the front door. The cedarwood beams across the ceilings and the shiplap walls. Sliding barn door accents. The built-in bookcases surrounding the brick fireplace.

It had been his grandfather's fondest hope one day they'd return to the ranch and settle there with their children. Had CoraFaye guessed what—who—Jack had on his mind when he was building the house? If so, it would explain so much regarding her current hostility.

A labor of love, he called it.

But he'd started building the house months before Kate arrived in Truelove. When they'd both believed they were long since divorced. So why would he build a house according to her tastes? Especially after how things ended between them.

Had things ended between them?

Kate's heart sped up, and she took the curve too fast, drifting over the yellow line. Sucking in a breath, she took her foot off the accelerator. Thankful there'd been no oncoming traffic, she eased into her own lane.

Distracted mountain drivers became dead mountain drivers. But this thing—she dared not put a name to it—between her and Jack had her completely discombobulated.

Reaching the base of the mountain, she breathed a sigh of relief as the land leveled out to slightly gentler terrain in the valley. Rolled hay bales dotted grassy meadows. Taking the longer, more scenic route into town, she drove past the Apple Valley Orchard with its row after row of leafed-out apple trees. Her heart pricked.

Blueberry picking wasn't the only thing they'd done with Liddy. They'd also gone on a fall apple picking excursion and hayride there one year. A sob caught in her throat. Once upon a time, she'd been happy here.

Why had she ever thought running away would make things better? She'd been in such pain. The kind of emotional pain that made it difficult to draw the next breath. The sort of pain she hadn't believed a person could experience and go on living.

Approaching the entrance to the rec center, on impulse she swerved into the parking lot. The swimming pool had hovered at the back of her mind since Saturday afternoon.

There weren't many swimming pools in the African bush. Zero, in fact. She'd kept her distance from pools since Liddy died. But she was so tired of being driven by fear. Groaning, she laid her forehead against the steering wheel.

Everything felt out of control. She'd lost Liddy. The cancer had returned. And then there was Jack…

What was she going to do about Jack?

Heart-sore, she scrutinized the sprawling, one-story brick building. As for swimming pools? This one thing she could face and conquer today.

Before she talked herself out of it, she swung open the door and stalked toward the entrance. Behind the reception desk, Miss ErmaJean glanced up, startled. The unmistakable aroma of chlorine permeated the air.

"Swimming…" she gasped. "Pool… Where?"

ErmaJean's denim blue eyes watered, but she pointed toward the end of the corridor.

Kate ran down the hall. Not stopping to consider she might be interrupting a lesson in progress, she yanked open the door and barreled inside.

But the pool wing was dark and deserted. Only the gentle lap of the water against the sides of the pool broke the silence. She'd taken her time driving back to Truelove after lunch with Jack. So it was much later in the afternoon than when AnnaBeth picked up Hunter on Saturday.

A not-so-small mercy. No one to witness her unravel. Although, ErmaJean had probably already notified the nearest mental health facility. And Gram.

One consolation, however. Given the state of rural health care, the nearest mental health facility wasn't exactly *near*. She had some time.

Venturing to the edge of the pool, she slipped out of her canvas sneakers. She rolled her jeans to her knees. She eased down, letting her feet dangle over the side into the water.

She wasn't sure how long she sat there. With a soft, gentle whoosh of air, the door opened and closed behind her.

Maggie inched down beside her. "Okay if I join you?"

"It's your pool." She shrugged. "I promise I wasn't about to drown myself."

Reaching behind her head, Maggie tightened her long, brown ponytail. "I didn't think you were. It's a peaceful place to think."

Kate's gaze swept the hunter green sport skirt and workout top. She didn't recall Maggie being so health-conscious and fit. Not that they'd known each other well. She and Jack had been three grades ahead of his cousin. In high school, the equivalent of dog years.

"I hear you're no longer an Arledge. Gram tells me you've married the new police chief."

A smile touched the recreational director's features. "A few years ago. It's Maggie Hollingsworth now." She gave Kate a measured look. "I hear there's a bit of a question as to your current surname." Her lips twitched.

Kate laughed. "True enough." There was no denying the irony of the situation in which she found herself with Jack.

Maggie's deceased grandfather had been GeorgeAnne's

and CoraFaye's oldest brother. *Note to self—try not to insult Maggie's family members.* Not too much of a hardship, except when it came to CoraFaye, of course. Although, Kate had long suspected the rest of the Allen-Arledge clan barely tolerated CoraFaye, either. And they were blood kin.

Maggie didn't seem driven to break the silence that fell between them. Kate was surprised at how comfortable she felt with her. In some ways, it was a relief to be with someone who already knew everything. From the glorious beginning of her life with Jack to its painful end.

As a teenager, Maggie attended Kate's wedding. As a young woman, she'd attended Liddy's funeral. Bringing Kate full circle to the niggling worry driving her to the pool in the first place.

She cleared her throat. "Do you teach the swim classes here?"

"I teach tumble classes for the preschoolers and a silver sneaker class, which your grandmother rocks, by the way. But we have a professional swim instructor from the athletic department at Ashmont College who moonlights at our center."

Kate jutted her chin. "There should be safety pamphlets in the lobby, or even a class for the parents on how to protect their children around the water."

"That's a great idea. I'd be willing to work through the logistics with you. I also teach a fitness class for pregnant women. You're a nurse-midwife, I believe."

"I am."

Maggie nodded. Her ponytail bobbed. "We could use more like you on our side of the mountains."

"I'm not staying in Truelove."

Maggie's brown eyes locked onto hers. "I see."

Kate wondered what exactly she did see. "I'm sure a

midwife would've been helpful when you and your husband—?"

"Bridger," Maggie supplied.

"—When you and Bridger had your children. I saw you at the Mason Jar the other day. Two little boys. Twins."

Maggie's face transformed. "Austin and Logan. They're turning five this week."

Same age as Liddy. Her stomach knotted. As Liddy would have been.

"The boys weren't born in Truelove." Maggie's mouth pinched. "They were born in Atlanta. Like you, as soon as I was able I left Truelove to pursue what I believed to be greener pastures."

"I see." She echoed Maggie's earlier remark.

"Probably not." Maggie gave her a small smile. "The boys have only been back in my life about three years. I gave them up for adoption when they were born."

Kate's mouth dropped. From the instant the delivery nurse placed Liddy into her arms, nothing could have pried her daughter away from her.

Nothing, except death.

Maggie fisted her hands. "I was attacked by one of my firm's corporate clients."

Kate gasped. "I'm so sorry. I didn't know."

"At the time, I couldn't raise them. No one knew, only Aunt Georgie. That's when I returned to Truelove. To try to forget."

Kate knew about trying to forget.

Maggie threw her a watery smile. "Or at least that was what I thought. God had other plans. It was Bridger's brother and sister-in-law who adopted the boys, but after their deaths, the twins came into Bridger's life. And when he became Truelove's police chief, they all came into mine."

Her heart went out to Maggie. She didn't know what

to say. What could she say? For the first time, she understood the dilemma others had faced in trying to offer comfort in the aftermath of Liddy's death. They'd meant well. At least, they'd loved her enough to try.

"We don't tell everyone about the boys. Just people we trust."

Kate looked up. "I would never breathe a word to anyone." She tilted her head. "You and I hardly know each other. I'm surprised you wanted to share your pain with me."

Maggie swiped at the tears on her cheeks. "You're easy to talk to."

"It's a nurse thing."

"Perhaps." Maggie sighed. "Or, I sense you might understand better than most. We have a lot in common."

"But I've never…"

Maggie peered at her. "We both understand what it means to suffer."

Kate reared a fraction. And then like a dam bursting, her story poured out. She couldn't have stopped had she wanted to.

"Drowning isn't like on TV. It was silent. No splashes. What takes place is mostly under the waterline. There was no noise. That was later when we were trying to save her. Our backs were turned for an instant. An instant was all it took. Drowning is the number one cause of accidental death in children under the age of four. Why didn't my pediatrician tell me? Why did none of the baby books I read warn me?"

Maggie took hold of her hand.

"I don't know why she left the poolside cabana where we were eating with the other SEAL families. Maybe because she was two and a curious child. The light was golden just before sunset. A sparkling, dancing path of liquid sunlight. We used to hike with Liddy in a baby harness to the top of Dolan Mountain. We'd stand there on the grassy bald at sunrise warmed by the rays of the sun on our face. She used to hold her hand to the light as if sifting it through her baby fingers."

Sobs racked Kate.

"Was Liddy trying to touch the light?" She'd never know what went through Liddy's mind that day. "Jack spotted her at the edge of the pool before I did. He raced toward her. She was reaching, stretching over the water. She lost her balance and fell, hitting her head on the cement step. She disappeared into the water."

Maggie's arms went around her.

"After that, I only remember snatches of what happened. There was chaos. I was screaming her name. Jack dove into the pool. Thirty seconds… No more and he got out of the pool holding Liddy's dripping-wet body in his arms. She was ashen."

Maggie held her tight. "Oh, Kate. Oh, Kate."

"We were surrounded by our SEAL family, every operator trained in the basics of emergency first aid. Jack laid Liddy on the concrete. Tyler, the combat medic in the group, immediately went to work on Liddy. My RN training went into overdrive. I spelled Jack and Tyler doing CPR." Kate stared at the far wall. "The first child I ever performed CPR on was my own daughter."

"You kept her alive."

"Long enough for the paramedics to arrive. They kept her alive long enough to get to the hospital where a machine took over. The doctor did a brain scan… She was gone. It was only the machine keeping her body alive. He talked to Jack and me."

Gaining control of her emotions, she gently released herself from Maggie's hold. "I kept thinking this was a nightmare from which I'd awaken. But I never did. I think now I never will."

"I'm so terribly sorry for what you've been through." Maggie gripped her hands. "Have you ever shared what you felt that day with Jack?"

Kate quivered. "No."

Maggie bit her lip. "I held what happened to me inside so long, I almost lost Bridger and the boys. But once I found the courage to say the words, it helped."

Kate stood up, her feet wet on the concrete. "Thanks for listening. I can't tell you how much it means…"

"Ditto for me, too." Rising, she dusted off her tennis skirt. "I'd love to have you out to the house so we could talk through the content of those water safety pamphlets. I'd have to get the boys occupied on their ninja warrior playset, but then we'd be free to talk on the porch where I could keep an eye on them. Unless seeing them would be too hard."

Kate stepped into her shoes. "Hard, but something I expect I need to deal with instead of running away as is my usual instinct."

"I have a summer intern, so I'm able to take off most afternoons to be with the twins. Would lemonade and cookies work for you one afternoon next week? I'll check my schedule and text you. Oh, fair warning. Puppies may or may not also be involved."

She laughed. "Two o'clock sounds perfect." Despite a sudden vision of curling up with a small dog in front of the fire at Jack's house, she wagged her finger at Maggie. "But taking home a puppy is not in my future."

Would that it were.

She drove past the Truelove welcome sign into town. Her car rattled over the bridge. She'd never seen the connection with Jack's cousin coming. She admired how

Maggie had overcome her own tragedy and made something positive out of something that began so terribly. It was high time she started thinking about how she could do the same.

Outside the police station, she spotted Maggie's husband in deep conversation with the mayor on the sidewalk.

Kate felt rather astonished at herself for sharing everything she'd kept locked inside. One more thing Gram had been right about. The longer she'd held it in, the worse it had been. But she felt better. Drained, but the building pressure had eased.

She looked forward to her playdate with the puppies. She'd gone into the rec center to face a fear and emerged with a new friend. She smiled as she passed the Jar, closed until morning, with its cheery red and pink geraniums in the window boxes.

Kate was meeting AnnaBeth there for brunch soon. Her social calendar hadn't been this full in years. After Liddy died she'd isolated herself, even from her colleagues in Africa.

Pursuing friendships had been too hard. Relationships too costly. Yet somehow she'd acquired two new friends in the space of a few short days. Three friends—if she counted this all-together new, unexplored terrain of friendship with Jack.

She turned into Gram's neighborhood. AnnaBeth and Maggie had caused her to rethink her opinion of Truelove. And, the kindness of people in a town where no one was allowed to remain a stranger for long.

Gram wasn't home. After storing the bucket of blueberries in the refrigerator, she put together a chef's salad for their dinner. That and Gram's homemade pimento cheese would make a fine meal. She found herself actually hungry for the first time in days.

She placed dinner in the fridge to stay chilled. Yet even after she set the table, there was still no sign of Gram. Filled with a restless need to do something, she spied the white cardboard box, sitting on the hearth exactly where she'd left it.

It was time. Her heart thudded. Well past time.

She carried the box to the sofa and set it on the coffee table. Palms suddenly slick, she yanked off the lid before she lost her courage. Perched on the edge of the cushion, she took a deep breath and reached inside. Her fingers encountered something soft, smooth and silky.

Heart in her throat—an anatomical impossibility but nonetheless true—she drew out a pair of tiny, white satin and pearl infant shoes. The shoes Liddy had worn for Kate's first Mother's Day. She clutched the baby shoes to her chest. And remembered.

All the days of Liddy's life couldn't have been sunny, but somehow in Kate's memory they were. She recalled the church service in Truelove, where they'd come to celebrate the women who'd been mothers to them. She remembered the feel of Liddy in her arms. The spicy, masculine scent of her husband, his shoulders brushing against hers in the pew…

"K-Kate?" Gram's voice wobbled. "Are you all right?"

Smiling, she opened her eyes. "I didn't hear you come in."

"IdaLee and Charles had me over for tea." Gram sank beside her on the couch. "You opened the box."

She cradled the small, perfect shoes in the palm of her hand. "I didn't get far."

Gram's wise, old eyes fanned out at the corners. "What's

important is you made a start." She made a move as if to go. "Shall I leave you to it?"

She placed her hand over her grandmother's wrinkled, blue-veined hand. "I'd love for you to stay." If she'd learned anything from earlier with Maggie, shared pain was halved pain. "Look through it with me."

"I'd be happy to keep you company, dear heart."

Other treasures emerged. A favorite, dog-eared storybook. A bright pink hair bow.

"Will you look at that?" Gram fingered the ribbon loops. "Do you remember the spring Liddy was here? She played in the garden, running along the paths between the daffodils and tulips. Pretty as a picture."

Kate smiled. "Later, she sat on the patio with us."

Gram nodded. "Her head bent over one of her picture books. This bow as pretty as one of the flowers. Like the flower the hummingbird believed her to be."

There'd been a flash of iridescent green and red as a hummingbird hovered over Liddy's bright pink bow. Realizing Liddy wasn't a flower, its wings whirring, the hummingbird soon dashed away.

"Such a beautiful moment." Gram's eyes shone. "A fleeting joy."

Her throat thickened. "Not unlike Liddy herself."

Gram squeezed her hand.

"It has never seemed right that objects outlast their owner." She sighed. "Grandpa's pipe. Dad's fishing pole."

"Because it wasn't ever meant to be that way." Gram brushed back Kate's shoulder-length hair. "But I take comfort in the fact I'll see Liddy again. We'll be reunited one day." Her wrinkled lips upturned. "In another better, eternal garden."

Since she'd returned to Truelove, she'd glimpsed the same faith in Jack. And instead of the anger she usually felt over the losses of her life, she yearned to know that kind of strength. That kind of peace.

Reaching inside the box again, she withdrew a white envelope containing a lock of Liddy's hair. She stroked the golden curl with the tip of her finger.

"I think that's all I can handle today," she whispered.

"Agreed." Gram slipped her arm around Kate's shoulders. "What would you think, dear one, about putting some of Liddy's things into a memory box?"

"Jack and I talked today about doing something to commemorate her life."

"Like a memorial service?"

She nodded slowly. "Maybe... I'm not sure. Something simple, though."

Gram gave her a hug. "No need to decide right now. You and Jack discuss it."

"I like your idea of a memory box."

Gram laced her hands together. "A borrowed idea. I saw a shadow box Callie Jackson at Apple Valley Orchard put together of little things from her wedding several years ago to Jake."

"Where would I go about getting something suitable for that?"

"Callie ordered it online." Her grandmother inched forward off the sofa. "I can get the link from her and order something similar for you."

Laying the golden curl inside the envelope, she got to her feet and helped her grandmother off the couch. "I'd love that. Thanks, Gram."

"No problem." Her grandmother waved aside her thanks. "Next-day delivery. I expect I ought to turn my attention to putting something together for dinner."

"Already done." She smiled. "Just waiting for you to get home."

"Thank you, sweetheart." Gram touched her cheek. "That was thoughtful of you. It's so nice to have you home for a spell."

Something stirred inside her heart. It *was* nice to be home. Home in Truelove.

Chapter Eight

The next morning, Kate had breakfast ready when her grandmother came downstairs.

In a pink floral top and cotton trousers, Gram sat down in the breakfast nook. "Aren't you bright and bushy-tailed this morning?"

She wasn't close to feeling bright, much less the human equivalent to bushy-tailed. The nagging headache and low-grade fever she couldn't seem to shake robbed her of energy, but she had no intention of living what remained of her life confined to bed.

"You slept through the last few nights without any nightmares." Gram reached for the juice glass. "Or at least I haven't heard you cry out."

"I hadn't thought about it." She sprinkled powdered sugar over the crepes she'd made. "But you're right." She set the plate adorned with blueberries in front of her grandmother.

"Looks delicious." Her grandmother smiled. "The Jack effect."

She chose to misunderstand. "These are the berries Jack and I picked the other day."

Gram gave her a reproachful look, but she cut into the crepe and took a bite.

Kate sat down. "Probably not up to Mason Jar standards, but how is it?"

"Delicious." Her grandmother surveyed Kate's empty place setting. "Have you already eaten?"

She didn't want to lie to her grandmother, but explaining the mere thought of food made her gag would lead to a conversation she wasn't ready to face. "I'm good."

"You aren't eating enough, Katie Rose." Gram pushed her half-eaten crepe across the table. "Finish mine."

Fighting the nausea that roiled her stomach, she took a sip of water. "I'll wait till I see Jack."

Her grandmother's features lit. "It's wonderful you're spending so much time together."

"Don't go reading more into it than there is, Gram."

Her grandmother stabbed a blueberry with her fork. "Your face glows with happiness after you're with him."

It was true. It had been wonderful to be with him again. They always had such fun together. She'd felt more like herself—her best and truest self—than she had since Liddy died. Thanks to Jack.

Neither of them were the same head-over-heels teenagers they'd been once upon a time. But she enjoyed getting to know the new, quieter, more mature Jack. She wouldn't have traded this time with him for anything in the world.

One day, after she was… Kate's grip on the glass wobbled… After she was gone, she prayed Jack would find someone to love him the way he deserved. She wanted him to know happiness again. He would make someone a terrific husband. Just not her.

After the chemo and many childless years of marriage, Liddy had been an unexpected gift. Someone else would eventually give him the child he so desperately wanted. The child she'd never be able to give him.

She set the glass with a small thud onto the table.

Gram looked up. "What's wrong?"

"Nothing." She dropped her gaze. "What're you up to today?"

"I was going to spray the roses, but—"

"You're mighty dressed up to spray roses in the garden."

Her grandmother carried her plate and juice glass to the sink. "As I was about to say, with the high winds advisory I think I'll leave that until tomorrow." She turned on the faucet.

Kate jumped up. "I'll do the dishes."

Gram waved her away. "You did the cooking. I'll do the cleanup. GeorgeAnne has called the girls to a meeting at the town hall. No excuse not to attend now."

The girls of the Double Name Club. Not one was under seventy years of age.

Biting off a smile, Kate leaned her hip against the island. "What are y'all planning now? A run for the White House? World domination?"

Gram sudsed a plate. "Jack has such a positive effect on your sense of humor."

Leave it to her grandmother to turn every innocent remark into a matchmaking ploy.

Gram rinsed the plate and a handful of silverware. "The gazebo committee has finally raised enough money to hire a carpenter who specializes in historic restoration."

She dried the dishes her grandmother set in the drainboard.

Gram handed her a glass to dry. "What're you and Jack doing today?"

"A trail ride." She darted a glance at Gram. "He was hoping you'd make him a blueberry cobbler."

Her grandmother smiled. "I think I could make that happen this afternoon."

Gram lifted the stopper out of the sink. The suds and water spiraled down the drain. "A trail ride sounds fun. It looks to be a gorgeous day. Just be careful driving up there. The wind can make the climb in elevation tricky."

Kate took her time getting ready. Not because she wanted to look her best for Jack. Of course not.

She frowned at her reflection in the bathroom mirror.

It would be silly to make a big to-do over seeing him. It was a dusty trail ride after all. But that didn't stop her from applying a touch of concealer to hide the purple shadows under her eyes. She dabbed a spot of blush on her cheekbones. She turned her head, evaluating the result. Better...

She'd never be that dewy-eyed girl with skin like a peach again, but not bad for a dying, thirty-three-year-old nurse who'd spent the last three years under a harsh African sun.

At that morbid thought, she smiled. Gallows humor. It was how she and many of her colleagues coped with the sometimes hopeless conditions they too often encountered.

She pulled on a pair of jeans and her old boots from the back of the closet. She shrugged into a cotton shirt the same color as the petals on Gram's lilac bush. Jack had always liked her in that color.

Planting her hands on her hips, she glared at herself. It didn't matter what color Jack liked or disliked on her. They were friends. More than she'd ever dared dream they could be again.

She scraped her hair away from her face and into a ponytail. Not leaving it hanging on her shoulders the way Jack preferred. "There," she told the mirror.

"Talking to yourself now?" She rolled her eyes. "You're not only dying, but losing it, too."

Grabbing her phone off the nightstand, she realized she'd neglected to charge her cell overnight. But she'd charge it in the car on the way to the ranch.

She took a brief detour into the backyard to breathe in the spicy scent of Gram's roses. Lifting her face to the sky, she relished the warmth of the midmorning sun on her skin.

A brisk wind ruffled her ponytail. Sending it flying straight out like a flag on the Fourth of July.

If the wind was noticeable in the valley, it would be especially strong on the ridge. She hoped this wouldn't affect their ride. But no matter how the day was spent, what was important was she spend it with Jack.

She plugged her cell into the car's portable charger and wended her way up the mountain. The wind buffeted her car. Her phone dinged with a message, but she dared not loosen her hold on the wheel to check it out.

With no other vehicles on the road—no one was foolish enough to be out and about, except her—she concentrated on keeping the vehicle hugging the yellow line.

Kate rounded the final sharp bend and, soon after, pulled off the road, driving under the crossbars of the Dolan Ranch. At the sight of Jack's black GMC parked next to CoraFaye's old Chevy, she braked and let the engine idle, torn by indecision.

She didn't relish a confrontation with his grandmother this morning. But berating herself for a coward, she forced herself to turn into the barnyard. Jack was probably bridle-deep in getting the horses ready for their ride. She'd lend him a hand.

Grabbing her half-charged cell, she strolled into the

barn. "Jack?" The scent of hay tickled her nose. Horses whinnied in their stalls.

She let her eyes adjust to the sudden change of light inside the barn. Several horses poked out their heads. Ambling toward the stable office, she paused to give each a gentle stroke. But the office was dark. No sign of Jack.

Remembering the new message, she fished her cell out of her pocket. Due to the advisory, he'd postponed their ride and headed over to Jonas's dude ranch next door to help him clear a downed tree, which had fallen on one of the cabins. An unoccupied cabin.

Putting away her phone, she sighed. She'd made the hazardous trip for nothing. If she'd remembered to charge her phone last night, she'd have gotten his message first thing this morning. Nothing to be done about it now—

A shaft of light blinded Kate as the outer doors to the barn were flung open. Throwing up a hand to shield her eyes, she caught a glimpse of a short, wiry silhouette with a long braid.

"He's not here." CoraFaye's cat's-eye glasses glinted in the light. "So much for whatever manipulation you planned for today, Princess."

Lips tightening, she moved past her. "No need to get your pigtail in a snarl, CoraFaye, I'm leaving."

Jack's grandmother grabbed her arm. "Haven't you done enough to him? Have you no shame?"

"Let go of me, CoraFaye." She twisted free of the older woman's grasp. "Get out of my way."

Arms folded across her skinny chest, CoraFaye stood her ground. "With him not around to defend your indefensible treatment, maybe it's better we have it out right now."

She sidestepped the woman. "I don't want to fight with you." She headed across the barnyard.

"Run away! That's your answer to everything, isn't it, Princess?"

"Stop calling me princess!" She did an about-face. "What part of leukemia and losing my child in any way resembles a fairy-tale existence to you, CoraFaye?"

"You are the most selfish…" Advancing, CoraFaye jabbed the air between them, punctuating her words. "Toxic. Emotionally psycho-needy human being it has ever been my misfortune to meet."

Kate rocked against a sudden downburst of wind. "How dare you."

"What's the plan this time, Princess?" CoraFaye jutted her scrawny chin. "How long do you plan to torture him with snatches of a happy future you and I both know you're incapable of fulfilling? How long before you run back to your clinic? Exploiting his feelings for you and then discarding him like yesterday's trash?"

Kate shook so hard she thought she might explode. "You don't know anything about him and me. About who we are."

"There is no 'we,'" CoraFaye spat. "Maybe I was wrong about you. Perhaps it isn't Jack you deceive, just yourself."

She took a backward step.

"If you ever truly loved Jack—" CoraFaye rounded on her.

Kate sucked in a breath.

"—you'd walk away now. This week or next month, we both know you'll leave him again. Let him get on with his life."

She squeezed her eyes shut.

"Do you intend to leave Truelove again? Answer me, girl. For once in your self-serving existence, tell the truth."

She stared bleakly at the older woman.

"Can you assure me you're here to stay?"

"No." Her voice sounded small. "I can't."

She loved Jack too much to let him suffer with her over what was coming.

Her headache, milder this morning, now raged heavy and severe. She felt the ache of her bones. Weariness settled upon her shoulders.

CoraFaye opened her hands. "Then please, Kate. I beg you. Stop dallying with his emotions. Make your peace with the grave and leave him be."

Her gaze locked onto CoraFaye's. The old woman knew not the full import of her words. A lifetime of broken promises and shattered dreams flitted through Kate's mind.

"I'm sorry, CoraFaye," she whispered. "For everything."

"So am I." His grandmother's bony face softened. "More than you'll ever know. I—"

A horn blared. A dark blue crossover barreled into the yard. Thrusting open the driver's side door, a statuesque redhead stumbled out.

CoraFaye's brows constricted. "Is that—?"

AnnaBeth clutched at her belly. Underneath her summery pink dress, water gushed down her bare leg. She staggered and fell to her knees. "Help me," she cried.

Kate had already started running toward her.

The wind howled around the eaves of the house. Kate and Jack's grandmother struggled forward against the bits of dirt stinging their eyes. It took them both to haul AnnaBeth upright.

"Your water's broken," Kate yelled to be heard above the wind.

"It's too soon," AnnaBeth screamed. "I'm only—" The wind snatched her words away.

"Let's get her inside!" CoraFaye shouted.

AnnaBeth moaned, almost going down again. Kate laid a hand on her belly. "She's in labor."

They did their best to shelter the pregnant mom from the worst of the storm front's fury. Battling the wind, the walk to the house felt twice the actual distance, but CoraFaye was stronger than she looked.

With one final push, she propelled Kate and AnnaBeth into the shelter of the screened porch. They half carried AnnaBeth into the safety of the kitchen.

The contraction eased, and AnnaBeth leaned heavily upon the counter. "Braxton Hicks." She rubbed circles on her belly. "I've had a lot of trouble with false labor."

"Nothing false about your water breaking," CoraFaye, ever the emphatic, retorted.

"You're not helping." Kate put her arm around Anna-Beth. "How long have you been having contractions?"

"I felt this tightness around my stomach when I got up this morning, but it went away. Like before."

She led her to a chair.

AnnaBeth shied away. "I'm such a mess. I can't sit on…"

"Hush." CoraFaye laid a dish towel over the seat of the ladder-back chair. "I'm not too old to remember birthing my children. Rest while you can. Between the pains."

Wincing, AnnaBeth sank into the chair.

Kate glanced at her wristwatch. "Have you timed the contractions?"

"After Jonas and Jack left—"

"They're not at your place cutting up the tree?" Cora-Faye shot a sharp look at Kate.

AnnaBeth shook her head. "The chain came off the chain saw. They went to town to get a part they needed at Allen Hardware."

CoraFaye glowered. "And you didn't think to mention to your husband you weren't feeling well?"

"I was feeling fine." AnnaBeth lifted her chin. "I had this incredible burst of energy. I hadn't felt that good in weeks."

"Burst of energy, huh?" CoraFaye cut another look at Kate. "Heard that one before, I 'spect."

Holding AnnaBeth's wrist, Kate took her pulse.

AnnaBeth nodded. "So I decided to clean the bathtub."

CoraFaye gasped. "You don't mean to tell me you climbed into the bathtub and commenced to scrubbing?"

"It needed doing."

CoraFaye folded her arms. "Nesting impulse."

"Be that as it may—" Kate released AnnaBeth's arm "—you are most definitely in labor. Where's Hunter?"

"He went to spend the day with his grandma Deirdre and Jonas's stepdad, Dwight. Oh—" A spasm of pain crisscrossed her features. She touched her hand to her belly.

CoraFaye's eyebrows arched. "Here we go again."

Kate looked at her watch.

The contraction easing somewhat, AnnaBeth half rose out of the chair. "I need Jonas."

CoraFaye grimaced. "You need a doctor."

"I was headed to Truelove to surprise him."

CoraFaye smirked. "You're gonna surprise him all right."

"But then there was this terrible pain. Stronger than any I'd felt before so I pulled in here."

"Good plan." CoraFaye nodded. "Head to the hospital in Asheville. 'Cept you're in no condition to drive, especially in these winds. I'll call Jonas to come get you."

Kate cupped AnnaBeth's shoulder. "Wasn't there a maternity ward in the regional hospital over the mountain?"

CoraFaye shook her head. "Closed last year. Not enough births in our rural county to justify keeping an obstetrician and labor-delivery nurses on staff. Only recourse for gynecological exams and child birthing is Asheville."

Kate scowled. "Asheville's an hour away."

Crying out in pain, AnnaBeth slumped into the chair, clutching the edge of the table.

"Take a deep breath in through your nose." Kate bent over her. "That's right. Now exhale. Good. Then two short pants and one longer blow out."

"Hee-hee-hoooooo. Hee-hee-hoooooo."

"Excellent." As the tautness of AnnaBeth's belly loosened, she reached for the soon-to-be mom's elbow. "I think we should move you somewhere softer."

AnnaBeth groaned. "I want Jonas."

"Let's get her to the guest bedroom." CoraFaye helped the young woman stand. "We're not going to make it to the hospital, are we?"

Kate shuffled AnnaBeth toward the hall. "No, we're not."

"What can I do to help?"

"Put your shower liner on top of the bed."

Seconds later, Kate heard ripping as the older woman yanked the liner off the hooks. With a firm grip on the expectant mom's arm, she walked AnnaBeth to the bedroom.

CoraFaye removed the comforter and spread the plastic liner across the bed. "I'll call Jonas."

"By all means do." Kate lowered AnnaBeth onto the edge of the mattress. "But first dial 911."

She helped AnnaBeth lie down. CoraFaye laid pillows to prop AnnaBeth into a semi-sitting position.

"I'm going to try to be very gentle," Kate told the young mom. "But I need to see how far you're dilated."

Moving aside, CoraFaye let her get on with it.

Kate sat back. "You're fully dilated."

"Jonas is supposed to be here," AnnaBeth wailed. "My mother is supposed to be pacing a hole in the floor outside the delivery room."

Keeping a determined smile on her face, Kate got off the bed. "Baby Stone has other plans. He or she is in a hurry to meet his or her mom."

AnnaBeth wrung her hands. "The contractions are close together, aren't they?"

"Labor is progressing hard and fast. I doubt the EMTs at the Truelove firehouse will make it here in time." She looked CoraFaye square in the eye. "Jack's grandmother and I will be delivering your baby."

The wind had picked up in intensity. Hailstones clattered against the old farmhouse. Kate jolted. CoraFaye should have returned by now.

Gripping the plastic liner in her fists, AnnaBeth moaned, seized with another sharp contraction.

"I'll be right back." Kate patted her arm. "I'm going to scrub up in the kitchen."

AnnaBeth clutched her hand. "I really need to push."

"Try not to push yet, A-B. Not until you can't resist the urge any longer." She extricated her hand from AnnaBeth's death grip. "Breathe through the next contraction and try to stay calm."

Worry for the old woman and concern for the mother-to-be gnawed at the outward professional calm she'd been trained to display no matter the situation.

She should have never agreed to let CoraFaye go out to the car for her midwife kit. She'd wanted to go herself, but CoraFaye insisted AnnaBeth needed Kate more. If anything had happened to Jack's grandmother, she'd never forgive—

Clothes and hair askew, CoraFaye burst into the kitchen, brandishing the small navy blue backpack. "A blessed coincidence, or do you always keep a midwifery kit in your car?"

Kate zipped open the backpack, checking her supplies. "Force of habit. Always had it freshly stocked in the jeep at the compound in Africa. Never knew when we might be called out."

She rolled her sleeves and scrubbed her hands to her elbows. "You should probably scrub up, too."

CoraFaye handed her a couple of paper towels. "And sing 'Row, Row, Row Your Boat' while I do?"

"Something like that." Lips twitching, she dried her hands. "I see where Jack gets his sense of humor. Let's leave the doors unlocked so the EMTs can get in quickly once they arrive."

"About that…" CoraFaye sighed. "The ambulance is en route, but they were finishing another emergency call farther afield than Truelove."

She hung the fetoscope around her neck. "How much farther afield?"

"The highway 'tween Truelove and the county seat." CoraFaye washed her hands. "The high winds turned two tractor trailers over like they were nothing but a bunch of matchbox cars."

Kate's eyes widened. "Casualties?"

"Minor bumps and bruises says Nadine at the firehouse. Some eedjit tourist also thought it would be a good idea to roast marshmallows in this wind." CoraFaye shook her head at the folly of flatlanders. "Set the national forest ablaze. Chief MacKenzie and the rest of his boys took the call to help the rangers put it out."

"So no help there, either."

"Kate!" AnnaBeth called.

"Coming!"

Jack's grandmother slung the backpack over her shoulder. "We're on our own till the paramedics arrive."

"Did you reach Jonas?"

"Racing toward us as we speak."

Kate slipped on blue disposable gloves. "For Anna-Beth's sake, I hope he gets here in time."

"Ready or not—" CoraFaye followed her down the hall "—that baby's a-coming."

Entering the bedroom, Kate plastered a big smile on her face. Positioning herself at the end of the bed, she checked the progression of AnnaBeth's labor and then laid a blanket across her knees.

CoraFaye pulled a chair next to the bed and sat down. "Hold on to my hand, sweetie pie. Squeeze as hard as you can. I'm pretty tough. I can take it."

AnnaBeth's body convulsed. "Hee-hee. Hoo-hoo."

Kate patted her leg. "I think we're ready to push now."

"Is that the proverbial royal 'we'?" AnnaBeth grumbled. "You sound like my mother."

Kate smiled. "You're doing great and about to be a mother yourself."

The wave of pain loosened. AnnaBeth's head flopped onto the pillows.

"Next time we're—"

AnnaBeth glared.

Kate's mouth quirked. "Next time, *you're* going to count to five during the contraction and then take a deep breath as soon as it's over."

"Until the next one, you mean," AnnaBeth growled.

"Such a trouper," CoraFaye cheered.

AnnaBeth went rigid. "Here it comes again!"

"Yell all you want to, sweetie pie." CoraFaye smoothed the hair out of AnnaBeth's eyes. "Nobody to hear you but the horses."

"One… Two… Three… Four… Five," AnnaBeth panted.

"Almost there," CoraFaye encouraged.

"Just a few more pushes."

Bent nearly double with the effort to put all her strength into it, AnnaBeth scrunched her face. With a final push, the baby slid into Kate's hands.

"You've done it!" She smiled at the young mother. "You have yourself a beautiful baby girl." She glanced at her watch. "Time of birth—twelve fifteen p.m."

CoraFaye hugged AnnaBeth. "Congratulations, sugar."

There was a commotion in the hall. Jonas clambered into the room. "AnnaBeth, are you okay?"

CoraFaye moved so he could get closer to his wife.

"Hello, new papa." Teary-eyed, AnnaBeth touched his cheek. "You've got a brand-new daughter."

Brow creasing, Kate's attention turned to the baby.

Jonas kissed his wife's forehead. "When can I meet this new daughter of mine?"

Heart pounding, Kate rubbed the baby's skin with a towel.

AnnaBeth stretched out her arms. "Can I hold her now, Kate?"

She tapped the baby's feet. "Not just yet…"

This couldn't be happening to another woman's child. Not again. Not on her watch. *Please, God…*

CoraFaye wrapped her arms around herself. "Oh, Kate."

AnnaBeth hitched up onto her elbows. "Shouldn't she be crying by now?"

Moving swiftly, Kate cut the umbilical cord and clamped it. "She isn't breathing."

AnnaBeth clutched her husband. "Jonas! Kate, do something."

She wrapped the limp, gray baby in the towel. "Cora-Faye, grab the Ambu bag for resuscitation out of my pack."

Kate got on her knees and laid the baby on the floor beside the bed. "You'll have to pump per my instructions."

Jack's grandmother frantically pawed through the contents of the backpack. "Got it."

"Put the neonatal mask securely over her face."

With CoraFaye at the baby's head and herself at the baby's feet, she pressed her two index fingers to the correct spot on the baby's tiny chest. "I'll push one-two." She pushed. "Squeeze the bag for one, CoraFaye."

CoraFaye's hand shook but she obeyed without hesitation.

Kate pushed to stimulate the baby's heart. "One-two."

CoraFaye squeezed the bag, forcing air into the baby's lungs. "One."

As if from a distance, she heard AnnaBeth's small whimpers. But her focus never wavered from the little girl fighting for her life. "One-two…"

"One," CoraFaye grunted.

The back-and-forth continued over and over again.

Someone laid a hand on her shoulder. "Kate."

Oblivious to everything but the child, she shrugged it off. "One-two."

"Kate."

She looked across the baby. "CoraFaye, you're supposed to—"

Jack's grandmother scrambled to her feet. A paramedic took her place.

"Let us take it from here, Kate." Luke, another paramedic she vaguely recalled owning a Christmas tree farm, eased her aside.

"How long?" the other paramedic asked.

Scooting onto her haunches to give the EMTs room to work, she blinked at him. "I don't know. I didn't have time to look."

"Ten minutes." CoraFaye put her hand to her throat. "I watched the clock. It was ten minutes."

"She's breathing on her own," Luke announced.

Thank You, God. Thank You.

AnnaBeth lunged forward. "She's alive?"

The other paramedic laid the baby on her mother's belly. "See for yourself, Mrs. Stone." He monitored the baby's vital signs.

"Well done, Kate." Offering his hand, Luke pulled her to her feet. "You kept her alive for us to get here."

Then Luke readied mother and child for transport to the hospital in Asheville. With the rattle of squeaky wheels, the EMTs pushed the gurney out of the bedroom.

Kate rubbed at her temples. The pain reliever she'd taken this morning had long since worn off. "Thank you, CoraFaye, for everything you did."

"I only did what you told me to do. You're quite something, Kate Dolan. If you hadn't been here today...?" Eyes glistening, CoraFaye seized her hands. "You saved the little girl's life."

"God saved her life," she whispered, her voice raw. "We had the privilege of seeing Him work."

CoraFaye had called her Kate Dolan. The two women held on to each other.

Her gaze flicking over Kate's shoulder, CoraFaye stepped away. "I'll make sure the boys have everything they need."

For the first time, Kate became aware of Jack in the doorway. His grandmother edged around him and into the hall.

When he looked at her like that… A warm, buttery feeling flooded her senses. "How long have you been standing there?"

His eyes aglow, a muscle jerked in his jaw. "Long enough, darlin'. Long enough."

Chapter Nine

Jack was proud of Kate. Never more so than today. She was such an incredible nurse.

Yet the sight of her on her knees saving the baby's life shook him. Triggering the memory of how he'd tried and failed to save Liddy. Jagged, raw emotions surfaced, tearing him apart inside.

But he couldn't give in to the storm brewing within him. Not here. Not now. Not ever. The fallout would be too devastating. Too complete.

After the ambulance left, Kate insisted on helping CoraFaye put the room to rights. He feared another confrontation between the two most important women in his life. But his grandmother, never one to hesitate stating her mind, remained uncharacteristically quiet.

He didn't feel right about Kate traveling down the mountain alone. He followed her vehicle to Truelove. Getting out of his truck, he walked Kate to her grandmother's porch. With her safely home, he turned to go.

"Wait. You're leaving?" A line puckered her forehead. "Come in. Stay a while."

He shook his head. "I—I need to see to the horses."

Kate saved Jonas's child. Why hadn't he saved theirs?

Why hadn't he, God?

Suffocating guilt rolled over him like a tsunami. How she must hate him. How he hated himself for failing her and Liddy.

"Can we do the trail ride tomorrow?" Kate frowned. "Jack?"

He edged away. "I should get back. Horses are probably spooked."

Running his hand over his head, he knocked his Stetson to the ground. He stared at it, lying atop Martha Alice's white azaleas. He made no effort to retrieve it.

"What's wrong, Jack?" She reached for him.

Breaking out in a cold sweat, he stepped off the porch. "T-Tomorrow." He'd agree to anything so long as he put some distance between them.

She plucked his hat off the azalea. "Aren't you going to take your—"

But he was already climbing into his truck. He slammed the door behind him. Reversing, he backed out of the driveway with a screech of his tires. Leaving Kate, hat in hand, blinking after him.

Now who was the one running?

At the ranch, the horses were fine. Munching hay, their heads bobbed over the stall door. Not nearly as spooked as Jack.

Tension ratcheted the knot in his gut tighter and tighter. He wasn't sure how long he could hold it together. Inside the farmhouse, he grabbed a few essentials from his bedroom.

His grandmother eyed the rolled sleeping bag he'd tucked under his arm. "Jack—"

"Don't." The ache in his heart intensified. Words would soon become impossible. His throat was closing fast. "I'll be at my house."

For once, she didn't badger him, but she did send a plate of chicken potpie with him. Leaving the stable in the capable hands of his assistant, he fled to the sanctuary he'd slowly crafted over the last three years.

In summer, the light lingered long. Gazing at the mountain, he sat in a folding chair outside the back door where one day he hoped to erect the deck. The shadows lengthened.

He watched the sun traverse the sky until the golden orb disappeared behind the ridge, bathing him in twilight. Only then did he force himself to head inside. His booted steps echoed in the empty house.

If he'd been a better father, Liddy wouldn't have died. If he'd been a better husband, Kate wouldn't have spent the last three years in Africa.

She wouldn't still be the deeply wounded woman she was today. It was all his fault. He'd robbed her of the opportunity for people like her grandmother who loved her so much to be there for her and help her heal.

He spent a sleepless night on his knees, wrestling with himself, with God and with blame.

Sometimes he went days without reliving the horror of the moment he pulled Liddy from the water. He felt again the building panic he'd experienced when it became clear she wasn't responding. With cold clarity, he recalled the instant he and Kate made the decision to take their beloved child off life support.

With an instinct as old as Eve, Kate had climbed onto the hospital bed to hold their child. If he lived to be a hundred, he'd never forget how she'd pressed her ear to Liddy's chest as her heartbeat slowly faded away.

Then, completely falling apart as he hadn't allowed himself to do that terrible, terrible day, he came unglued, crying out. And he wept.

His ability to shut down his emotions to do what was essential had saved his life and that of his team countless times as a SEAL. His stoicism against the waves of grief and guilt had not served him so well as a husband in the face of their indescribable loss. Well-intentioned to not add his burden to the heavy weight of the grief she already bore, shutting down on Kate had ultimately proved marriage-ending.

Yesterday, instead of being there for her, he'd walled himself off from Kate again.

When dawn's golden rays streaked the sky over the mountain, he knew seeking God's forgiveness for his failure wasn't all he needed to do. It was time to seek Kate's.

On automatic pilot, he went through the usual morning turnout. Feeling the worse for wear, he nevertheless plowed through the riding regimens and feeding schedule with the trainer. When the first riders arrived at 8:00 a.m., he'd already put in what most would consider a full day's work. But owning a stable wasn't a job. It was a lifestyle.

Around nine, Kate texted him, asking if he'd be able to carve out any time today for their postponed trail ride. A request easily accomplished. After letting her down in the most fundamental of ways three years ago, he wasn't about to disappoint her now. But fatigue, physical and emotional, gnawed at him.

He texted her to come around two o'clock. He had Fancy saddled by the time she arrived.

She handed him his hat. "I gave it a gentle brushing to clean off the dust."

He could barely look at her. "Ready to ride?" He settled the hat on his head.

She smiled. "I can't wait."

Her smile broke open his heart. Giving place to emotions he had no right to feel. A happiness he didn't deserve.

They left the barns behind. Letting her get used to being in the saddle, he didn't say much. He appreciated her not asking him about why he'd left Truelove so abruptly yesterday.

Riding side by side along the trail, only the jingle of the harness and birdsong broke the quiet of the afternoon.

"I don't blame you for being angry with me, Jack."

He swung around. "Why do you think I'm angry with you?"

She gestured at the space between them. "You haven't had much to say."

"I'm not angry with you." He turned back to the direction in which his horse plodded. "Would you want to hike to the summit of Dolan Mountain? Retrace our steps with Liddy?"

"A remembrance walk." Kate sighed. "She loved those hikes with us. I'd like to see it one more time."

Or did she mean one last time? Heaviness like a stone settled in the pit of his stomach.

Reaching the jumping-off point, they dismounted and secured the horses. The tangy scent of spruce wafted through the air. Keeping to the faint deer trail, they climbed toward the top through the evergreen forest. Despite the confession he dreaded, with each step he took up the steep, rocky path, a bit more of the tension coiling his gut eased.

Dolan Mountain wasn't really a mountain, but one of the grassy ridges found in the southern part of the Appalachians, locally known as a bald. Still the change in elevation, about twelve hundred feet, was enough for him to feel the tug on his leg muscles as they ascended.

"Hold up, Cowboy." Emerging out of the trees, she slumped against a giant boulder. "I need a moment." Her hand on her chest, her lungs straining to replenish her oxygen, she took a few deep breaths. "I don't hike as often as you."

"I haven't been here in a long time." He kicked a stone, sending it clattering back the way they'd come. "Too many memories. Couldn't do it without you and Liddy."

"Then it was right we do this together."

He glanced at her.

She was having more trouble catching her breath than he would've reckoned considering she'd always been outdoorsy. Or at least the Kate he used to know. "Are you sure you're up for it? You seem—"

"I'm fine." Grimacing, she pushed upright. "We've come too far to turn back now."

As applicable to their marriage as to the hike. But for Liddy's sake, he'd agreed not to push that issue. Not until after the memorial service.

Kate hadn't mentioned contacting their lawyers, which gave him hope they could find their way to a more satisfactory closure.

Would she stick around long enough for him to address the elephant between them? All the more reason to apologize while he had the chance. *Stop procrastinating.*

He turned back to the trail. She followed him through the dense tunnel of rhododendron bushes. The overgrown, intertwined branches formed a towering arch over their heads, blocking the sky and sun. The temperature immediately cooled.

Jack waited for her to catch up. "Glad to see you brought a jacket."

Untying the denim coat from around her waist, she slipped her arms through the sleeves. The grassland summit was a good fifteen degrees cooler than the ranch, even in summer. Leaving the canopy cover behind, they bridged the remaining distance to the high bluff.

At the massive display of purple rhododendron and orange flame azaleas, his heart hitched.

"It's as beautiful as I remembered in my dreams," she rasped, grabbing his arm.

She was as beautiful as he remembered in his dreams, and he was so thankful to be able to share this with her.

The vastness of the panoramic view never failed to move him. To the west of the spectacular vista lay Tennessee. To the east, North Carolina. On a clear day like today, the undulating folds of the Blue Ridge fanned out around them.

It was a place set apart out of time. Since the first Dolans arrived in these mountains, for generations his family had stewarded this environmental treasure.

Kate sat on one of the large, flat boulders dotting the grassy overlook. Plucking an open-throated, purple blossom off a rhododendron, he sank down beside her. He threaded the flower behind her ear.

She smiled at him. For the first time since she'd returned to Truelove, he detected a glimmer of peace in her gaze. He hated to shatter the moment, but he was choking on the words he needed to say.

He knotted his hands and summoned his courage. "I want to apologize for failing you when Liddy died."

"You have nothing to apologize for." Taking a ragged breath, she scanned the horizon. "We failed each other, Jack."

"I shut down."

She looked at him. "I ran away." A gentle breeze blew a strand of hair across her cheek. "If anyone should apologize, it's me."

Because he couldn't help himself, he brushed the tendril out of her face. "Aren't we a pair?"

A smile flitted at the corners of her mouth. "That we are."

He took a small comfort from her use of the present tense. Probably a slip of the tongue. There hadn't been a "them" for a long time. But he wasn't done yet with the apologizing.

"I also need to ask your forgiveness for not saving Liddy." He shook his head. "I understand why you ran away. I don't blame you. I can't forgive myself."

Her eyes widened. "I don't blame you for what happened. You did everything humanly possible to save her."

"If we'd never gone to the pool party—"

"Don't think I haven't wondered the same thing. It was an accident. A terrible accident."

"I was her father. It was my job to keep her safe." Blood pounded in his temples. "I've agonized over not protecting her. After all my training—"

"No one can control everything." She squeezed his arm. "You were a wonderful father. Liddy adored you."

He tore his gaze away, unable to face the truth of what they'd become. Of what he'd done to them. "You must hate me." He swallowed.

"Oh, Jack." There was a resignation to her voice. "I couldn't hate you if I wanted to. Which I don't. You should know me better than that."

His eyes cut to hers. "I feel I don't know you at all. Sometimes I wonder if I ever did. I wonder if I imagined what we once were to each other. Were we the real deal, Kate?" He cocked his head. "Or was it wishful thinking on my part?"

"You didn't imagine… Our love was true."

"Was." His gaze bored into hers. "The greatest regret of my life besides losing Liddy is losing you, Kate."

Her lips trembled. "I've missed you, Jack. So much."

"And yet I never heard from you. Three years, Kate. Three years." Fighting for control over his emotions, he lifted his hat, crimped the brim with his hand and settled it on his head. He turned away. "We should head—"

"Kiss me."

He whipped around. "What?"

"I want you to kiss me."

The wind played havoc with her hair. She was playing havoc with his heart.

"I don't think that's a—"

"We are the real deal, Jack. No matter what happens after Liddy's service..." Her voice broke but she rallied. "Just once more." She touched his forearm. "You wanted us to remember. Let's remember who we were... Who we are, Jack. Please. Kiss me."

This was a bad, bad idea. But he could no more deny her than he could deny his desperate need to hold her in his arms. Once more.

Just one more time.

"Oh, Kate..." His hand settled on her waist as it had when they danced at their wedding. He drew her closer into the circle of his arms.

Leaning forward, he let his lips brush across her mouth. He stopped. Giving her the chance to pull away.

But she didn't.

Her forehead resting on his, she murmured his name. His heart turned over in his chest. He closed his eyes.

She clung to him. "Jack..."

And he kissed her again.

The pain of the past fell away. The uncertainty of the future didn't exist. All that mattered was that she was in his arms. And she was his beloved wife.

How he still loved her.

The realization rocked him. His anger toward her was

nothing but a self-protective mechanism to blunt the raw edge of losing her. But he wanted more. So much more.

Jack wanted a life with her. *Was that even possible, God?* Could he change her heart? Convince her to stay? Get her to see they were better together than apart? Surely for her to have kissed him like she did, she must love him, too.

His emotions surging like a runaway horse, he pulled away from her. If he didn't stop now, he never would. He was a different sort of man from the one who'd pursued her so relentlessly when they were younger.

She wrapped her hands around the nape of his neck. "We aren't finished."

Jack pried her hands free. "I think for now we are."

Her face fell. His words had hurt her, but this was about so much more than today. He needed to take the long view.

Finding the way back to her heart. She was worth fighting for. They were worth fighting for.

He held her hands against his chest. Surely she could feel the rapid beat of his heart. "We agreed to focus on the anniversary first."

She glared at him. "Friends…" She made a face as if the word tasted unpleasant.

He laughed, his chest rumbling beneath her palms. "We can talk more about this later." He kissed her fingers. "After the tree-planting service."

A stricken look crossed her face. "Later?"

"Just a few more days." He smiled. "It's not so long."

She slipped her hands free from his grasp. "Not long at all." Inexplicable tears formed in her eyes.

He reached for her but she stepped away. "What's wrong, darlin'?"

She shook her head. "We need to think through Liddy's service."

They talked all the way to the stable. But he couldn't shake the nagging feeling something else troubled her. Something he didn't understand.

And not knowing made him afraid.

Kate found her grandmother deadheading roses in the garden.

"You're back." Gram swiped a forearm across her brow. "How was the trail ride?"

"Good?"

Her grandmother laid the pruning clippers into the wicker basket at her feet. "You don't sound so sure. What happened?"

She gestured at the spent rose petals inside the basket. "I didn't mean to interrupt."

"The older I get, the more I feel the heat. I work a little. I rest a lot." Gram balanced the handle of the flower basket on her arm. "If you want to tell me what happened at the ranch, I'd be glad to listen. If it's none of my business, I won't be offended."

She'd been shaken by Jack's humble plea for her forgiveness. If anyone needed to be forgiven, it was her. CoraFaye was right. She was despicable for leaving Jack to deal with the aftermath of their child's death on his own. For failing to be there for him.

As for the kiss… The kiss had shattered everything she believed to be true about herself. And them.

She sank onto the garden bench. "Jack blames himself for what happened to Liddy."

Gram perched beside her. "Do you blame him for not saving Liddy?"

"No." At the memory of their kiss, her lips tingled.

"Or at least, no more than I blame myself for getting distracted."

Removing her floppy sunhat, Gram fanned her face. "Liddy adored both of you. I never met a happier child. Protecting our children is a natural instinct, but there will always be things out of our control to prevent."

"I think it's more than that with Jack." She threw out her hands. "Because he was a SEAL, he somehow feels his child should've never drowned. He feels the weight of his guilt at such a deeply personal level."

"Like most men, I daresay, he has a need to fix what's broken." Her grandmother ran her fingers through the petals in the basket. "No surprise, he's heaped blame after blame upon himself. He must learn to forgive himself."

Kate massaged her forehead. "It's such a mess. Jack and I... We're both such a mess." The headache had become unremitting. She didn't have to be a medical expert to realize she was getting worse by the day. "We're broken beyond repair."

"I do not believe anyone is broken beyond repair. You know my thoughts on where to find the source of the comfort you so desperately seek, but I'll say no more on that subject. However..." Gram cleared her throat. "The time grows short."

Kate went still. "What do you mean?"

"What would you and Jack like to do for Liddy's memorial?" Her grandmother's eyes narrowed. "What did you think I meant?"

"Nothing." Reaching behind her head, she wound her hair into a makeshift bun. "I've been thinking about how to honor Liddy's life. Jack calls it her 'legacy.'"

Gram nodded. "Anything specific you'd like to do?"

"We talked about the ceremony today..." Among other things.

Cheeks burning at the memory of his lips, she trailed her gaze over the nodding columbines and pink dahlias. "Jack had an idea about sponsoring one of the oak trees on the green. What do you think?"

"It would be a wonderful tribute."

"Maybe we could have a dedication service." Kate bit her lip. "I'd like to invite friends to share memories of her."

Her grandmother's eyes moistened. "I think that's a lovely idea. I could help you create a list of people to invite, if you'd like me to."

"Yes, please. We'd also like to put Liddy's name on a plaque in front of the tree. Jack said he'd get someone to make it."

They went inside to get iced tea. At the kitchen table, Gram jotted down the names of local friends who'd known Liddy or had a connection to the Breckenridge-Dolan families.

"Jack's aunt GeorgeAnne." Her grandmother wrote with a flourish. "ErmaJean, of course." Gram and Erma-Jean had been garden buddies for years.

"Maggie is Jack's cousin so we should include her dad, Bridger and his mom, too." Kate traced the path of condensation down the glass with her finger. "But I don't think we should invite the twins. I'm not sure I can handle other children being there."

Her grandmother reached across the table for her hand. "I think that's a wise decision. It will be an emotional occasion."

"I don't want to offend Maggie, though."

Gram patted her hand. "I'll explain when I issue the invitation. But I believe everyone will completely understand." She returned to her list. "Who else?"

"Jonas is also Jack's cousin. So let's include his mom,

her husband, AnnaBeth, but not Hunter." She rubbed her eyes. "I'm sorry. This is getting ridiculous." With a screech, she slid back her chair. She fumbled to open the bottle of a pain reliever. "I can't seem to do anything right—"

Gram held out her hand. "Let me open it for you."

Handing it to her, Kate sat down. With a dexterous twist, her grandmother opened the bottle and spilled several white tablets into Kate's open palm. Tossing the pills down her throat, she guzzled tea to wash them down.

"That headache of yours…" Gram gave her a concerned look. "You've been taking a lot of pain medication. Maybe you should see a doctor."

Seeing a doctor was absolutely the last thing she wanted to do. Once she did, her grandmother wouldn't stop until she badgered out Kate's true condition. What with the confusing tangle of emotions brought on by seeing Jack again and planning the wrenching memorial for Liddy, she didn't have the strength to shoulder telling Gram she was dying, too.

Kate just couldn't face Gram's devastation until after the tree-planting ceremony.

"Pollen counts must be high." Not exactly a lie. Not exactly the truth. "What is it this time of year, Gram? Grasses and weeds or trees?"

"Grass, I expect." Her grandmother glanced at the notepad. "IdaLee and Charles?"

The diversion proving a success, Kate took an easier breath. "I wouldn't dream of leaving out a matchmaker. Come one, come all."

Gram's lips quirked. "Truer words."

"And then there's CoraFaye to consider. She's liable to have an objection, or three, about what we've planned."

Her grandmother's eyebrow rose. "You let me deal with CoraFaye."

Kate and CoraFaye had reached some sort of mutual peace agreement yesterday after AnnaBeth went into labor. She wasn't foolish enough, however, to believe the accord would last. Yet it also didn't seem right to exclude the older woman from the planning.

"We must include her." Kate sighed. "CoraFaye is Liddy's great-grandmother, too."

"I'll get her input but—"

At the sound of a car in the driveway, Gram peeked out the window. "Speaking of you-know-who…"

Kate blinked rapidly. "CoraFaye's here?"

The bottom dropped out of her stomach.

Chapter Ten

Kate gaped at her grandmother. "What could CoraFaye possibly want?"

Gram's mouth twitched. "Should I tell her you're unavailable?"

Kate squared her shoulders. "It's probably better if I hear what she has to say. I'll answer the door."

"Should I give you five minutes and then interrupt? Or shout out the code phrase, and I'll come to your rescue."

Kate cocked her head. "What code phrase?"

Gram's eyes twinkled. "Something along the lines of 'the terrier has landed.'" She placed her hand against her ear as if holding a listening device. "I repeat, 'the terrier has landed.'"

The doorbell rang.

"How about 'when pigs fly'?" Tears winking out of her eyes at her own hilarity, her grandmother clutched the countertop for support. "Or—"

"Gram!" She fluttered her hand. "Stop. Making. Me. Laugh."

She hurried to the front of the house. The door between the kitchen and the dining room swung shut behind her, and she couldn't help but smile at the echoes of her proper librarian grandmother laughing herself silly.

Maybe Gram had the right idea. Laughter might be the best medicine. She hadn't felt this good since leaving Africa. Then, she opened the front door.

"Took you long enough." Scowling, CoraFaye pushed into the house.

"Please…" Gritting her teeth, Kate closed the door behind her. "Do come inside."

Gripping the strap of her shoulder bag, CoraFaye glared at her. "Jack told me about the memory box you're putting together for Liddy."

She folded her arms across her chest. "Okay…" What burr did CoraFaye have up her saddle now?

"What exactly are you putting into this box?"

Kate arched her eyebrow. Surely the name itself was self-explanatory. She didn't have the energy or the inclination to fight CoraFaye today. *Give me patience.*

She took a breath. "Liddy's hospital wristband when she was born. A lock of her baby hair." She rattled off the items. "Photos of her first birthday party. The vintage, plastic pink jelly sandals she adored—"

"You're including happy memories you shared with her." CoraFaye blinked behind the cat's-eye glasses.

Unsure where Jack's grandmother was going with this, she nodded. "Yesssss…"

CoraFaye stuck out her bony chin. "Liddy and I shared some happy times together. Like that weekend you and Jack left her at the ranch to celebrate your anniversary in Charleston."

Unwinding slightly, she motioned the older woman toward Gram's front room. "Let's sit."

Stiff as an ironing board, CoraFaye settled on the edge of the blue brocade sofa.

Kate took a seat opposite her in the wingback chair. "I'd forgotten about that weekend."

"I had not." CoraFaye sniffed. "With y'all living in Virginia, I didn't get to see as much of Liddy as I would've liked. But I'll always remember that weekend... Jack's grandfather loved showing her around the farm."

"Liddy thoroughly enjoyed herself." Kate smiled. "She talked about nothing else for days. Feeding the horses. Picking wildflowers in the meadow."

"That was with m-me." CoraFaye's voice cracked. "We took a walk in the woods. It meant so much to me. I believed we'd have all the time in the world—years—but that weekend was all of Liddy I'd ever get. All any of us would ever get." Fighting tears, she finished in a near-whisper.

Before Kate considered the many reasons justifying her dislike of Jack's grandmother, she took the older woman's trembling hand in hers. "I'm sorry, CoraFaye."

And by sorry, she meant so much more than just the loss they shared of Liddy but also for the lost years before and since. For shutting out CoraFaye, deserved or not, from so much of her life with Jack. Truth was, they were both too much like cats.

Territorial. Circling each other. Constantly rubbing each other's fur up the wrong way. Their poor relationship was as much her fault as CoraFaye's.

Her gaze flicked to Kate. "I wondered if you'd allow me to contribute something to Liddy's memory box."

The sadness, the grief, the aloneness in those eyes— so like Liddy's—cut Kate to the quick. Going through the box of Liddy's life had begun a healing journey for her. How selfish would she be to deny Liddy's great-grandmother the same peace?

"I'd love for you to share something in the box, Miss CoraFaye."

Some of the starch left CoraFaye's spine. "Really?"

"What did you have in mind?"

CoraFaye opened her purse and withdrew an azure feather. "Liddy found this on our walk that day on Dolan Mountain."

She leaned forward. "A bluebird feather?"

"We picked and pressed wildflowers that morning. That afternoon we made my granny's famous tea cake recipe." CoraFaye handed the small feather for Kate to examine. "Liddy wore it tucked into her hair all day. Said the blue was just like her and her daddy's eyes."

"Yours, too, Miss CoraFaye."

A fond smile lifted the dour face Jack's grandmother usually presented to the world. "Yes. Like mine."

"But Miss CoraFaye, this is precious to you." She tried to give the feather back to her. "Are you sure you want to put this in the box?"

"I'm sure." CoraFaye patted her hand. "It's right that Liddy should have it. If only in the box of our memories of her."

Leaving the feather on the chair, she dropped to her knees in front of CoraFaye. Jack's grandmother's eyes widened.

"Thank you, Miss CoraFaye." She hugged the older woman. CoraFaye stiffened. "This means so much that you'd part with this treasure for Liddy's sake. And I know it will mean just as much to Jack."

"You're welcome." Relaxing a notch, she gave Kate a brief pat. "No need to get carried away, though."

Swallowing a smile, Kate got off the floor.

CoraFaye rose as well. "I'd best be getting back. The blueberry jam won't make itself."

Kate walked her to the door. "No, ma'am."

"AnnaBeth's mom is taking me to see baby Violet at the hospital in Asheville since I don't drive in traffic."

"They're calling her Violet? I love it." Kate smiled. "Is she doing all right?"

"Right as rain. The both of 'em." CoraFaye paused on the threshold. "But you know how them doctors are."

"I'm sure the hospital is keeping them a few days as a precaution."

"Victoria, AnnaBeth's mom, said we'd 'do' lunch." CoraFaye made a face. "Whatever that means. Like we're friends or something."

"I'm sure you and Victoria will have a lovely time."

CoraFaye bristled. "Don't know why that fancy flat-lander wants lunch with me."

She couldn't resist teasing the older woman. "We can't ever have too many friends, can we?"

Jack's grandmother snorted. Sun, moon, seedtime and CoraFaye. In a world where change was constant, it was good to know some people never did.

CoraFaye looked down the bridge of her glasses at Kate. An amazing feat considering Kate topped the tiny woman by a good six inches.

"Some of us don't have all day to go gallivanting 'round the countryside." Jack's grandmother wagged her finger. "Some of us have to work for our living."

"Yes, ma'am."

CoraFaye stalked down the porch steps. "Keep me in the loop when you work out the details for the ceremony." Flapping her hand over her shoulder, Jack's grandmother marched toward the old Chevy.

Kate resisted the urge to salute. "Will do," she called.

"Is it safe to come out now?" Gram hissed from the interior of the house.

"Some rescuer you are." Kate rolled her eyes. "The terrier has left the building. I repeat. The terrier has left the building."

Grinning, Gram came out onto the porch. "You were doing just fine without me. What did she want?"

Kate explained about the feather.

"That was kind of her." Gram's gaze took on a far-away gleam. "Would you be open to allowing me to share something meaningful at the ceremony to honor my memories of Liddy?"

"Of course." Kate hugged her arm. "I'm sorry I didn't think to invite you and CoraFaye to do so earlier."

Gram stepped into the house. "I've had this idea. Saw it at a memorial service for an old college classmate of mine a few years ago."

Kate followed her inside. "How can I help?"

"I've got this." Gram waved her hand. "It only requires a phone call and an expedited delivery."

Kate refilled her glass with iced tea. "What are you planning?"

Gram took a sip of tea. "Do you remember how much Liddy loved chasing butterflies?"

As her grandmother outlined her contribution to the ceremony, Kate did indeed remember a summer's day in Gram's garden with Liddy. In recalling the sweet memory, a little more of the ache eased from her heart.

Over the next several days, the final details of the tree dedication service came together. Summer camp had started. Jack was super busy so they talked mainly over the phone.

But Saturday evening, he took her to dinner at a swanky place in Asheville where no one knew either of them. A non-Liddy, new memory, which Kate thoroughly enjoyed. From the terraced balcony table, the sunset view was magnificent. Getting to know each other again, they talked and laughed for hours.

She could feel another piece of her heart succumbing to the wonderful man he'd become. No matter what happened after the ceremony next week, she'd treasure this evening with him forever.

Kate still wasn't ready to go to church with Gram on Sunday, but that afternoon she made time to visit baby Violet, recently released from the hospital, at the Field-Stone. With a shock of chestnut curls and deep green eyes, the baby was as lovely as her mother. AnnaBeth introduced Kate to her mom, Victoria Cummings. To her embarrassment, Victoria wouldn't stop thanking Kate for saving AnnaBeth and her granddaughter.

The Charlotte society queen was petite and rail-thin like CoraFaye. But unlike Jack's style-challenged grandma, with delicate pixie features, large brown eyes and a sleek cap of short, brown hair, Victoria was a picture of tropical summer elegance. She was also passionate about the lack of available health care in rural Truelove.

"We're going to have to put our heads together and see what we can do for our Truelove friends." Victoria waved her hands. She did a lot of talking with her hands. Gold bracelets jangled on her wrists. "CoraFaye has told me so much about you."

Kate could well imagine what the acerbic CoraFaye had said about her.

"CoraFaye is a hoot." Victoria smiled. "I like her."

"That is certainly one way to describe her," Kate conceded. But Victoria didn't put on airs, and Kate found herself liking AnnaBeth's mom, too.

On Monday, Gram's package arrived on schedule. Kate went through the last of Liddy's belongings in the box. More often than not, it left her tearful, but Jack had been right to urge her to go through the contents.

Seeing them helped her face the reality of her loss, but touching the things Liddy had loved also brought her a great deal of joy. She finished putting together the memory box that night. She had only to get through Liddy's memorial service the next day.

The morning dawned bright and clear. The sort of morning Liddy would have loved. Gram left early with ErmaJean to finish setting up the arrangements at the square. Jack had asked Kate to ride to the ceremony with him. Exactly as it should be. Liddy's parents, remembering and celebrating her life together.

It was a quiet, short ride to Main Street. Reaching over the seat, he held her hand. She was grateful for its strength and warmth. Her joints hurt like she had the flu. But she refused to let anything, even her worsening condition, keep her from this special day dedicated to Liddy.

Jack helped her out of the truck. "I'm nervous this morning. Words don't come easy for me. Silly, huh?"

"A man of action is more your style," she teased, hoping to lighten the moment. He almost smiled as they looked across the square at the site where the ceremony was due to start soon.

"There are things I want to say. Important things." Standing at her elbow, his deep voice rumbled through her chest. "I want to say them right for Liddy's sake."

"You'll do fine." Kate squeezed his hand. "I believe in you."

Filtered through the canopy of the remaining oaks, sunlight dappled the green lawn. Dotted along the four sides of the square were smaller trees, already dedicated by other Truelove families. Those saplings were dwarfed by the original trees. But they would grow and flourish, God willing, for a century more.

Most of their invited guests were already on the square when she arrived. Liddy's spindly, little tree sat in the middle of a larger hole, dug by the Parks and Rec Department. Shovels, borrowed from everyone in attendance today, leaned against the rough bark of the adjacent enormous oak. Parks and Rec had left a pile of dirt nearby to backfill the tree in the hole during the ceremony.

Jack leaned to whisper in her ear, close enough for her to feel his breath on her cheek. "Will you be okay if I mingle and thank everyone who's come? Or I can stay—"

"Go." She let go of his hand. "I need to do the same. But when we start…" She bit her lip.

"I'll find you." He gave her a crooked smile that set her heart aflutter. "We're in this together."

Nodding, she watched him go over to Jonas. Except for weddings and funerals, the mountain dress code was casual. This wasn't a funeral, but a celebration.

She'd dressed in a simple, pink sheath dress and black, low-heeled sandals. Like most of the men, Jack had worn jeans. But he'd exchanged his everyday Stetson for the taupe-colored cowboy hat he reserved for special occasions.

Maggie's husband, Bridger, had set up the chairs in several rows on the lawn closest to the little tree. Platters of cookies from the Mason Jar lined a refreshment table. Truelove never allowed an event to go unmarked by food. Food was how Truelove residents showed their love.

She went over to thank Kara for her kindness. The chef had discovered Liddy's favorite dessert was cinnamon chip cookies and insisted on catering the ceremony, free of charge.

A remembrance table held photos of Liddy with her

family—Jack, Kate, Gram, CoraFaye and both deceased great-grandfathers. Miss IdaLee had furnished the lacy tablecloth. Miss ErmaJean put together the beautiful flower arrangement of lacy-capped blue hydrangeas from her own garden. Surrounding the centerpiece, the bright yellow envelopes contained Gram's special surprise for Liddy.

From birth to death, small towns showed up for their people. And for everything in between.

She found herself touched by the contributions of so many to this special day. An indication of their love for Liddy and Jack. For her, too?

At a signal from Jack, she excused herself from GeorgeAnne and headed toward the little tree where he waited for her with Reverend Bryant. Walking toward them, she experienced a moment of déjà vu. Once a long time ago, she'd done the same on their wedding day in Gram's garden. CoraFaye and Gram took their places on the front row.

Reverend Bryant opened with prayer. "Today, O Lord, we remember Lydia Dolan's home-going…"

Struck by his choice of words, Kate opened her eyes. She'd never considered Liddy's death a home-going. She'd always viewed it as a leave-taking from her and Jack.

"…We thank You for Lydia's life. We ask You to bless her parents and those who loved her as we come together to celebrate her life," Reverend Bryant prayed.

It was odd thinking of Jack having a pastor, but he'd told her how the reverend had helped him through some of his worst times after Liddy died. Once today was over, Kate needed to come to terms with her own death.

Gazing over the bowed heads of those who grieved with them, she envied their faith and the strength that came with it. As a teenager living with Gram and Gramps, she'd been an indifferent churchgoer.

Reverend Bryant had been new to his pastorate then. She hadn't known him well. From what Jack had told her, he didn't seem like the kind of man who'd be shocked by her questions about the God who'd allowed her to suffer through childhood leukemia and the death of her daughter. Perhaps it was time she got to know the reverend better.

"Amen." Reverend Bryant adjusted his glasses. "The Dolan and Breckenridge family would like to thank everyone for your kindness through the difficult days since Lydia went home. Jack and Kate have a few words they'd like to say."

Widening his stance, Jack clasped his hands in front of him. "No matter how long or how short a time a person lives, we believe Liddy was born to us for a reason." His voice choked and he looked at his boots.

She twined her fingers through his. "Jack and I wanted to find a way to take the love we had for Liddy and transform it into a beautiful legacy."

He lifted his head. "It is our hope that in planting this tree we can bridge the memory of her life into the new life we must build without her." His Adam's apple bobbed in his throat.

Reverend Bryant opened his hands. "Kate, I believe there was something else you wanted to share?"

Scanning the sea of faces—new friends and those who over the years like Gram who'd loved her so much—she nodded. Gram clutched a white handkerchief to her streaming eyes. Sitting ramrod straight, CoraFaye's eyes were none too dry, either.

Kate raised her face to the sky, feeling the warmth of the morning sun on her cheeks. "Daddy and I miss you,

Liddy." She fought past the tremble of her lips. "Al-always."

"Courage," Jack whispered in her ear.

She refocused on the others. "Liddy was a happy, sweet, wonderful little girl. She could be a spitfire—"

"Not unlike her mother," Jack said.

Everyone laughed, including Kate. She offered him a grateful smile. How had she ever made it three years without him in her life? How would she ever face the remainder of her life—however short—without him? But she couldn't bear to think of that. Not now. Today was about Liddy.

A firm grip on her emotions, she turned to the crowd. "Curious and lively, Liddy was always into something and up for any adventure. This last, greatest adventure—" Kate looked at the sky "—she has started without us, going on before us." She swallowed. "Miss CoraFaye?"

Rising from her seat, Jack's grandmother angled toward the gathering. "Liddy's love of life was infectious. You couldn't help but smile when she was around. She was a kind and loving child. She always wanted to know everyone's name and be everyone's friend. Marth'Alice?" CoraFaye sat down.

Gram stood up. "She loved giraffes, sunflowers, ponies, chocolate bunnies and spending time with her family." After she resumed her seat, CoraFaye patted her arm.

Reverend Bryant placed his hands upon Kate and Jack's shoulders. "You honor your child best by healing. Your love for her will live forever."

She blinked back tears. In facing and accepting the loss of her beloved Liddy, there was healing. Never forgetting, but letting her go. Home. To Liddy's truest home. It was time. She was ready.

Oh God, I'm sorry for pushing you and everyone else

away. Please help me find the peace Gram and Jack have known. Thank You for Liddy. Whatever the future holds for me, I want to honor her by healing.

Jack glanced at her with concern, his hand tightening on hers. A deep emotion had seized Kate. But when she opened her eyes there was a lightness there, a peace, he hadn't seen since Liddy died.

Reverend Bryant moved toward the small bronze plaque the Parks and Rec Department had erected in front of the little tree. "Dedicated to the memory of Lydia Mae Dolan," he read.

The pastor handed a shovel to Jack. "As we watch this tree grow, we will remember you, Lydia. We will be reminded of the beauty your life brought to the world and to us."

Jack shoveled dirt into the hole around Liddy's tree. He passed the shovel to Kate, and she did the same. Jonas passed out the rest of the shovels. Jack and Kate moved aside.

Each friend or family member deposited their own shovel of dirt around the tree until the hole was covered, the roots buried and life for the tree could begin again.

Only in a new place. Like his precious Liddy.

He supposed the ceremony to be over, but Martha Alice handed out a batch of yellow, origami-style envelopes he hadn't noticed before. Yellow had been Liddy's favorite color. The color of sunshine and happiness.

Exactly what his daughter had been to him.

Kate gave him an envelope. He glanced at the words engraved on the outside. *Lydia Mae Dolan. We will always love you.*

"What's this?"

Her beautiful eyes gazed deeply into his. "Forgive

yourself, Jack. If there was ever anything to forgive, Liddy and I already have."

Forgiveness. Possibly one of the most beautiful words that existed. Something coiled tight in his chest loosened.

Reverend Bryant spoke a few words about the symbolic release of the butterflies in the envelopes.

Liddy had loved butterflies. He cut his eyes at Martha Alice, who smiled at him through her tears. On his pastor's mark, everyone opened the envelopes. There was a split-second pause, and then dozens of monarch butterflies emerged.

With a flutter of brightly painted orange-and-black wings, they rose skyward. For a few moments, the butterflies lingered, hovering above them, filling the air with the brush of their wings. They flitted across the space from person to person, one landing on a leaf of Liddy's small tree. Finally, as if one entity, they ascended higher and higher.

He watched them go, his face like the others, upturned to the sky. It was time. Time to let go of the weight of his guilt.

"Goodbye, my Liddy," he whispered.

As the wind sighed through the branches of the trees, he could almost hear Liddy's delightful little laugh. Emotion clogging his throat, he listened until he could no longer hear it. Until he could no longer catch a glimpse of the butterflies.

"Kate," he rasped.

Taking one look at his face, she pulled him behind the screen of a large tree trunk.

"Oh, Jack." She wrapped him in her arms. "Oh, my darling."

He'd always believed he had to remain strong for her and everyone else. He'd never allowed her or anyone to see his vulnerability. But the rough bark against his back, he allowed her to hold him. To see his frailty. To see the depth of his pain.

Jack's tears were a strange, bittersweet mixture of sadness and joy. But in their release, he felt as free as the butterflies. *Thank You.*

Life, birth, death. All of it good. Because even in death, there was always God.

Chapter Eleven

Kate spent the rest of the day with Jack.

At first, he seemed embarrassed by what happened at the tree-planting ceremony. He'd always kept his feelings locked tight within himself. But by letting her into his pain, he'd never appeared as strong.

She'd never respected him more. She was ready to admit it to herself, if to no one else—she'd never loved him more. And that scared her more than the cancer. If she didn't leave Truelove soon, she might never be able to leave him at all.

Kate lay awake for hours that night, contemplating what she should do, where she should go. She could no longer postpone telling Gram about the return of her cancer. She could hardly bear to think about saying goodbye to Jack.

The next morning, her heart was heavy when she dragged herself out of bed. A sudden wave of dizziness forced her to sit on the side of the bed while she got dressed. Negotiating the stairs, she clung to the railing.

In the kitchen, Gram looked up from her gardening journal. "Can I scramble you some eggs, dearest?"

Kate put her hand over her mouth. The notion of food

made her woozy. "No, thanks." She grabbed a water bottle from the fridge. "We need to talk."

Gram tilted her head. "What's on your mind?"

Unscrewing the bottle cap, she took a sip of water. As soon as the liquid hit her throat, she knew she'd made an awful mistake. Stomach heaving, she raced for the bathroom.

"Kate!"

Gram found her curled on the floor of the bathroom. Bleary-eyed, she looked at her grandmother. "Dry heaves," she whispered. Almost worse than the real thing.

"What's going on, Kate?"

"I'm so sorry, Gram." She moistened her lips. "The leukemia is back."

Shock, fear, disbelief and a dozen other emotions shone from her grandmother's eyes. Cutting into Kate like shards of broken glass. She'd have done anything in the world not to have burdened her grandmother with this terrible news.

"You have nothing to be sorry about, Katie Rose." Gram took a ragged breath. "Let's get you settled more comfortably on the sofa."

Gram fed her ice chips. After the nausea passed, her grandmother managed to get her to swallow fever-reducer pills.

"How long have you known?"

Kate sighed. "I started feeling horrible the day I flew out of Africa back to the States."

Perched on a corner of the seat cushion, Gram feathered a strand of hair out of Kate's face. "What is your white blood cell count?"

"I don't know."

Gram's forehead creased. "But what have the doctors said about your prognosis?"

"I haven't seen a doctor yet."

"Kate—"

"I won't go through chemo again." She pushed away the cup of chipped ice. "I refuse to let the brunt of this fall on you, Gram, the way it did on Dad and Mom."

"Honey, you must have a plan."

"I've done nothing but think about this since I realized something wasn't right inside me." She looked at her grandmother. "My end-of-life plan is for palliative care only."

"But you're a young woman." Gram grabbed her hand. "We will fight this."

She winced at the fierce strength in her grandmother's grip. "I'm tired, Gram."

Her grandmother's eyes blazed. "Jack won't let you go without a fight."

"Which is why I'm leaving Truelove tomorrow."

Her grandmother gasped. "You mustn't cut yourself off from everyone who loves you. You'll need a support network."

"You and I know what's coming." She swallowed. "I can't—I won't—drag Jack through that heartache. He's already endured so much after losing Liddy."

"Jack would want to be with you." Gram's mouth trembled. "He loves you."

She turned her face into the cushion. She couldn't think about that. She mustn't think about that. Because if she did, she'd lose her nerve in doing perhaps the most unselfish thing she'd ever tried to do for someone else.

"I can see you've already made up your mind." Gram's voice was brittle. "Where do you intend to go wait for this lonely death you've planned for yourself?"

"The children's cancer center in Chapel Hill has my records." She reached for her grandmother's hand again. "It shouldn't be too difficult to transfer into their adult ward."

Gram's hand felt cool and dry. "You're not going to walk out of that man's life again without saying goodbye, are you?"

She inched up on the pillow. "I'll tell him goodbye this afternoon."

Gram pursed her lips. "He deserves to know why you're leaving."

A conversation that promised to be excruciating.

"No more secrets. I'll tell him why, Gram."

"Good." Her grandmother rose. "I'd best see to packing a suitcase."

Kate caught her arm. "I don't expect you to come with me, Gram."

Her grandmother shot her a look worthy of CoraFaye. "If you think for one moment I'd ever allow my girl to spend her last days relying on the kindness of strangers, you better think again. Of course I'm going with you."

Tears swam in Kate's eyes. "I love you, Gram."

Her grandmother placed a light kiss on the top of her head. "I love you, too. But you'd best be ready. This time, Jack won't allow you to go so gently."

Kate fell asleep on the sofa. A few hours later, she woke feeling stronger. The house was quiet. Sitting up, she found a note next to her phone on the coffee table. Gram had gone to the supermarket on the highway to get a few travel supplies.

Picking up her phone, she saw she'd missed a handful of messages from Jack. When can I see you? she texted him.

After several moments, he replied. Name the time and place. I'll be there, darlin'.

She could almost hear the dragged-out drawl of his

voice. Her grandmother would be occupied for a couple of hours. Glad for the unexpected privacy, she asked Jack to come to the house. He promised to arrive shortly.

Kate went upstairs to fix her hair and put on makeup. Despite her best efforts, she looked haggard. She shrugged into a sweater. All of a sudden, she felt so cold.

Unable to get warm, she drifted outdoors into the garden to wait for him. Texting him, she let him know she'd be in the backyard. She sat on the bench next to the fountain. Preparing to break his heart. Again.

It wasn't long before she heard the creak of the garden gate. She stood up as he ambled over. His smile about broke her heart. A kaleidoscope of memories that would never become reality tumbled through her mind.

She fought the overwhelming urge to run her fingers along the nape of his neck and into his hair.

"We need to talk, Kate."

"Not yet." *Oh, please, not just yet.* She shivered. "Would you hold me, Jack?"

He threw her the lopsided smile that caused her insides to melt. "It would be my pleasure." His gaze swept over her, sending a flutter down to her toes. As always, she fit into his embrace like she'd been made for him. The buzzing in her head quieted.

Brushing her hair off her shoulder, his hand dropped to her arm for an instant. Butterfly-light, his gentle caress set her heart ablaze. Leaning closer, his hand made a slow trek to the small of her back. He smiled. She tilted her head.

He smiled. "I believe it's your turn to kiss me."

For a long blissful second, she forgot to breathe. Their breath mingled, her mouth only an inch from his, then she kissed him. Her hands cupped the back of his head. He sifted her hair between his fingers.

One final kiss to last her the rest of her life. A kiss for the ages. Like their love. If she truly loved him, she must set him free. But first, she must hurt him to save him from further pain.

Hardening her resolve against the battle raging in her heart, she pushed out of his arms. "I'm leaving Truelove tomorrow."

"No." Confusion and longing warred in his eyes. "We were supposed to talk about this, Kate. What does this mean for us?"

"There is no 'us,' Jack. There can't ever be."

"I thought you were happy in Truelove."

She had been. She was.

"I believed you were happy with me."

She wrapped herself in the sweater. "Please don't make this worse than it already is."

Anger sparked in his eyes. "How much worse can it be for me than you running away again? Running from the life we could build together." He reached for her.

She sidestepped his hand. "I'm not running away." If he touched her again, she'd be lost. "I can't give you the life you're dreaming of, Jack."

"Is this about Africa?" He took a step toward her. "We can work through this, darlin'. Please don't go."

"This has nothing to do with Africa. My mind is made up. There's nothing to discuss."

"I love you, Kate."

"Don't say that." She put her hands over her ears. "You're in love with a woman who no longer exists."

"That isn't true. I see you, Kate." He grabbed her hands and pulled them away from her ears. "And I love what I see."

"You can't love me." She jerked free. "I won't let you."

"I won't let you give in to your tendency to self-

-lacerate. I get that you're scared. I'm scared of trying and failing again, too. But we're so much better together, baby, than we are apart."

She shook her head. "Why do you make me say things that will only hurt you?"

A muscle jumped in his cheek. "If you were honest with yourself, you'd admit you love me. You couldn't kiss me like you did if you didn't love me. Say it, Kate. Tell me you love me."

"I don't love you, Jack," she yelled. "I won't."

His mouth flattened. "What about the last two weeks? Has this been some sort of game to you?"

"No... I—I—"

"Just give it to me straight." His eyes turned stormy. "Tell me why you won't give us a chance. In simple language that even a stupid cowboy like me can understand."

"There can be no future for us." She met his gaze head-on. "The cancer is back. I'm dying."

Stunned, Jack stared at her. Of all the things he'd thought she might use as an excuse, he'd never expected that.

Random comments, moments he hadn't understood, suddenly fell into place. This was what he'd sensed she was hiding from him. His heart shattered into a million pieces.

God, where are You?

This couldn't be happening. Not again. After all they'd survived, he couldn't lose her now. Somehow without quite realizing it, he'd taken her into his arms. And this time she let him.

"You won't go through this alone. I promise you, Kate." Her skin was warm to his touch.

Like the SEAL he'd been, he was already sizing up the situation. Formulating strategy. Working the problem.

"Wherever you need to go for treatment, I'll go with you."

She was shaking all over like a beech tree in a summer gale. "N-noooo…"

He'd hire a barn manager. His family and friends would rally to help him with the ranch. Jonas. Zach. Aunt Georgie would be there for his grandma.

"We'll spend every minute together, Kate."

"I—I d-don't want you to suffer, t-too." Her teeth chattered.

"We'll fight this, Kate."

Knowing how much her suffering would hurt him, perhaps irretrievably this time, Kate knew she had to do something drastic.

He rested his chin atop her head. "I won't let you die."

She wrenched herself out of his grasp. And said the unforgivable. "You didn't stop Liddy from dying. What makes you think you'd save me?"

Dropping her hands, he reared. Heat licked his cheeks as if she'd slapped him. And the look in his eyes…

Forgive me, Jack. I had to find a way to make you let me go. I'm sorry. Sorry for everything.

The distant throbbing of her temples had become an all-out assault on her senses. But there was no going back to what she'd thrown away. No going forward to a future that for her would never exist.

"I—I don't feel good, Jack," she gasped.

Overcome with sorrow, darkness nibbled at the periphery of her vision. Pitching forward, she fell into blackness.

Chapter Twelve

Jack caught her in his arms. "Kate!"

She moaned.

Cradling her, he sprinted toward his truck. After gently laying her across the seat, with a screech of tires he headed toward the only medical professional he could think of in Truelove—Dr. Jernigan.

When he stormed inside the pediatric office carrying Kate in his arms, the handful of children and their parents in the reception area looked up.

Amber, Dr. Jernigan's nurse, set a patient's file on the counter. "What's happened to Kate?"

"She collapsed," he panted. "I didn't know where else to go. You've got to do something to help her."

The petite blonde turned to the receptionist. "Get Dr. Jernigan into Exam Room Three stat." The middle-aged woman picked up the phone.

Amber ushered him down the corridor. "This way." She pushed open the door with her hip. "Lay her on the examining table."

Under the fluorescent lighting, Kate appeared even paler than she had on the street. Fear lacerated his heart.

The lanky, distinguished doctor in his late fifties hurried into the room. "What happened?" He hustled over to the table.

"We were talking. She said she didn't feel well."

Dr. Jernigan touched his hand to Kate's forehead. "She's burning up. Amber, let's see how high it is. Check blood pressure, too."

Amber pressed an infrared thermometer to Kate's forehead. "One hundred and four."

Other than a slight tightening of his lips, the doctor didn't respond. Jack had enough medical training in the Navy and as a dad to know that was high. Extremely high. "What's wrong with her?"

Amber wrapped the blood pressure cuff around Kate's upper arm. "Jack, let us work."

He swiped his hand over his head. "Just help her. Please."

Removing the stethoscope from around his neck, the doctor listened to Kate's heart and lungs. "Breathing is shallow. Lungs appear uncongested. Her heart rate is accelerated."

He pushed forward. "What does that mean?"

Dr. Jernigan reslung the stethoscope around his neck again. "BP?"

Amber took the cuff off Kate's arm. "One seventy-eight over ninety-eight."

Jack paced the small room. "Is it because her cancer has returned?"

Dr. Jernigan's gaze sharpened. "What cancer?"

"When she was a child, she nearly died from leukemia before she went into remission. But it's been almost twenty years."

The doctor and Amber exchanged a look.

"Cancer survivor. I didn't know that." Dr. Jernigan had only opened his practice in Truelove a few years ago.

Jack swallowed. "She did her treatments at the hospital in Chapel Hill where her family lived back then."

The doctor stuffed his hands into his white lab coat. "Amber, please have Peggy call the EMTs at the firehouse. She'll need to be transported to the hospital in Asheville."

"Asheville?" He stopped in front of the doctor. "That's an hour away. Can't you treat her here or at the hospital over the mountain?"

The doctor sighed. "I'm sorry, Jack. I'm a pediatrician, not an oncologist." He rubbed his chin. "They at least might be able to help her."

"Might? You're giving up on her? You can't let her die." Jack balled his fist. "Do something," he growled.

"We don't have the resources to help her or the laboratory facilities to run the proper diagnostics. Neither does the satellite facility over the mountain. I'm sorry, Jack, but she's better off in Asheville."

Amber tugged his arm. "You're not helping. We need to get her prepped for transport."

"Is there someone I should call?" The doctor continued to monitor Kate's vital signs. "To drive you to Asheville."

Jack burred up. "I'm not leaving Kate. I'll ride in the ambulance with her."

"There won't be room." The doctor looked at him. "I'm canceling my afternoon appointments. We can reschedule the well visits." He nudged his chin at Amber. "I'll ride along just in case..."

"In case what?" He went cold. "You think her heart might stop on the way to the hospital?"

The doctor didn't answer, but what he glimpsed in Dr. Jernigan's eyes did nothing to allay his fears. "Time is of the essence, Jack. Let us do what we can."

Deflating, he allowed the pediatric nurse to tow him

toward the reception desk. Amber asked Peggy to contact the firehouse.

With Peggy on the phone, Amber explained the situation to the parents and children waiting to see the doctor. Jack was glad of the solid weight of the counter. His legs felt as wobbly as a newborn colt's. The underpinnings of his life were being knocked out underneath him.

It wasn't thirty seconds later, he heard the wail of the ambulance. The firehouse was only a few blocks from the medical office building. Nothing was too far away in Truelove. Except, apparently, for lifesaving medical care. He sagged against the counter.

Two EMTs hurried through the door, rolling a gurney. Amber directed them toward the corridor. They pushed past him, the wheels of the cart squeaking.

One of the EMTs was Luke Morgan, Dr. Jernigan's new son-in-law. The pediatrician had recently married the young Christmas tree farmer's widowed mother. Seeing Luke, an absurdly sweet memory drifted across Jack's mind of the Christmas he'd gotten leave to spend the holiday in Truelove with his wife and chubby toddler. He, Kate and Liddy had spent a wonderful morning picking out a Christmas tree for Martha Alice's house.

Was he about to lose the only person who remained of his happy little family?

The EMTs emerged with Kate. An oxygen mask over her nose and mouth obscured her features. Crying out, Jack reached for her.

Amber took hold of him again. "Just a precaution. They didn't want her to have to labor so hard to breathe."

She kept a firm grip on him as they loaded Kate into the waiting ambulance.

Dr. Jernigan joined them on the sidewalk. "I've called ahead so the ER will be ready for us." He climbed inside.

Sirens blaring, the ambulance sped away.

Amber fluttered her hand as the chief of police's cruiser pulled next to them at the curb. "Here's your ride."

Jack glared at her. "You called the police?"

She jabbed her forefinger at him. "You're in no condition to drive to the Mason Jar, much less Asheville. Don't worry about Miss Marth'Alice. I'll make sure she gets there, too."

Bridger unfolded from the vehicle. "I'm driving you, Jack." He leaned his long, big frame against the open door. "I'll run my siren. We'll get there almost as quick as Luke. Give Amber the keys to your truck."

Not stopping to question why, he fished out the keys from his jeans pocket, placing them in Amber's outstretched hand. He got in the car.

Bridger took the winding switchbacks to the highway with a precision and skill born of his training. Once on the highway, the SUV gained speed and ate up the miles to Asheville. Bridger didn't speak, leaving Jack to his own thoughts. For which he was grateful. Consumed with worry, he stared out the window as the countryside flew by.

Soon, although not soon enough for Jack, Bridger pulled to a stop outside the ER. "I'll park and then find you."

Jack looked at him. "Thank you."

Bridger gave him a short nod. "Go. Take care of your lady."

Grabbing the handle, he flung himself out of the police cruiser. The doors of the ER whooshed open. He ran through the entrance. The pungent scent of antiseptic assaulted his nostrils. He didn't see Kate, Luke or Dr. Jernigan anywhere.

"Excuse me." He barreled over to the information desk. "An ambulance should've arrived with my wife."

"The ambulances have their own entrance." The woman squinted at him. "Jack? CoraFaye Dolan's grandson?"

He wiped a hand over his eyes. He recognized her from church. One of the deacon's wives. A lot of people made the trek into Asheville every day. Work had never been plentiful in the Blue Ridge.

"My wife." He leaned across the desk. "Where is she? Can I see her? Can I speak to her doctor?"

"Your wife?" The lady frowned and then her expression cleared. "Oh, of course. Kate." Reddening, the woman dropped her gaze and tapped a few keystrokes on her computer. "Is it still Dolan?"

Being from Truelove, the woman would remember he'd been single the last three years since returning home. In a small town, everybody knew everybody else's business, or at least believed they did.

"Yes." He clenched his jaw until his teeth ached. "Her name is Kate Dolan."

Kate might not think of herself as still his wife, but legally that's exactly what she was. If she and God would give him the chance, he'd make sure her name remained Dolan.

"The ambulance arrived moments ago." She punched a few more keys. "The attending physician will be doing an initial assessment. If you'd wait over there—" she motioned toward a row of chairs "—I'll tell the nurse to have the doctor give you an update as soon as they've got your wife admitted. It could be awhile, though." Her face softened. "I'm sorry to hear your wife is unwell, Jack. I'll be praying for you both."

Her kindness reminded him of why there was no place

he'd rather be than Truelove. Small towns might be nosy, but they cared for their own.

Feeling a hand on his shoulder, he turned.

Bridger nudged him toward the chairs. "Let's sit for a spell."

Over the next half hour, every time the automatic doors separating the waiting room from the triage section opened and medical personnel in blue scrubs ventured forth, Jack rose out of the chair. But after a while with no sign of Dr. Jernigan or any other physician coming out for him, he stopped getting up. Leaning his elbows on his jeans, he held his head in his hands.

"Why don't they let us know something?" he grunted.

Bridger repositioned the regulation hat on his knee. "They won't talk to us until they have something to tell us."

Was she fighting for her life? After everything he and Kate had endured and lost, was he going to lose her, too? The idea of a world without her gutted him.

I'm struggling here, God. I barely survived Liddy's death. Please don't take Kate, too.

At a bare whisper of sound, he turned his head. Bridger's eyes were closed, but his lips were moving. He and Bridger didn't know each other well, but he found himself unbelievably touched the rugged law enforcement officer would pray for Kate. And he vowed when she emerged from this crisis healthy again, he would do his utmost to be a better friend to Truelove's youngest-ever police chief.

"Your boys like horses?"

Bridger's eyes flew open. "What kid doesn't?" His forehead crinkled. "Why?"

Jack steepled his fingers. "Would they enjoy learning to ride horses?"

Bridger sat back. "They'd love that, but you don't have to do that because I'm here with you today."

"I know, but I want to. You and Maggie have done a good job with them." Jack placed his arms on the armrests. "How old are they now?"

At the mention of his wife, Bridger lit up. Jack figured he did the same with Kate.

"Thank you. They're five. Starting kindergarten in the fall."

Five.

Jack's smile slipped a notch. He hadn't made the connection before, although he was sure Kate had. He had it straight from the proverbial horse's mouth—Aunt Georgie—that Kate had made an effort to befriend Maggie Hollingsworth. Kate was braver than she gave herself credit for. Peer milestones were tough for a bereaved parent.

Liddy would have been the same age as Austin and Logan. Would they have been friends?

It suddenly occurred to him Bridger had faced his own challenges in overcoming Maggie's reluctance to pursue a relationship with him due to the traumatic event in her past. Yet now, they were the epitome of happily-ever-after.

He sighed. "How did you do it, man?"

Bridger cocked his head. "Do what?"

"Convince Maggie to give you a chance?"

"I won't kid you. It wasn't easy." His gaze took on a faraway look as he turned some memory over in his mind. "But worth it. You have to be prepared for the long haul. Patience, love and—" Bridger cut his gaze at the entrance doors sliding open "—a matchmaker or two didn't hurt, either. Speaking of double-named women…"

"What?"

Chuckling, he patted Jack's shoulder and stood up. "Ladies."

As he glanced over his shoulder, Jack's eyes widened. It appeared the entire contingent of the Double Name Club had turned up. Including his grandmother and Kate's.

Bounding out of the chair, he met the two halfway across the waiting room.

Always brimming with youthful vitality, Martha Alice looked as old as he'd ever seen her. "What's happening with my girl?"

He took her hands in his. "We're waiting for the doctor to give us a status report. They're still assessing her, I think."

Jack darted a look at his grandmother. She wasn't known for coming any farther off her mountain than Truelove. "Did you drive Miss Marth'Alice here, Grandma?"

His grandmother didn't look in much better shape than Martha Alice. If he didn't know what a tough customer CoraFaye was, he'd have sworn in a court of law she'd been crying.

"Grandma?"

The older woman looked haggard. "You know I don't drive in traffic. Your cousin drove us over as soon as GeorgeAnne called AnnaBeth."

"I don't see Aunt Georg—"

"She's helping Jonas park," Miss ErmaJean offered. "AnnaBeth wanted to come, too, but with the newborn…"

He could well imagine his bossy aunt "helping" Jonas park his truck.

Martha Alice's mouth trembled. "It's bad, isn't it, Jack?"

He wished he could give her better news.

When he didn't say anything right away, her shoulders drooped. "I was so afraid something like this was going to happen."

He let go of her. "She told you her cancer had returned?"

"Only this morning." Kate's grandmother swayed.

Grandma put her arm around Martha Alice. Would wonders never cease?

"Kate promised she was going to tell you."

She did tell him. Right before she collapsed. He scrubbed his hand over his face. The entrance doors slid open again, and it seemed half the population of Truelove strolled inside.

Maggie went straight to her husband. "Any news?"

"Not yet."

Miss IdaLee and her husband, Charles, arrived on the heels of the pastor.

Jack did a quick headcount. "Is there anybody left in Truelove?"

His cousin Jonas schlepped in behind the always-brisk GeorgeAnne.

"Let's get everyone settled." The organizational genius—a.k.a. the one with the talent for bossing people around—took charge as hospital personnel began shooting the crowd pointed looks. "We've activated the prayer chain. Those remaining in Truelove are minding the children. And baking casseroles, of course."

Jack was glad to have someone else do the wrangling. A feat not unlike the herding of cats. Bridger touched his arm. "Jack." He cleared his throat.

He swung around to find Dr. Jernigan and a lady doctor waiting to speak to him. Like flicking a light switch, the Truelove group went quiet.

"Jack, this is Dr. Amira Patel." Dr. Jernigan performed the introductions.

Her arm still around Kate's grandmother, CoraFaye came forward with Martha Alice.

"Is my granddaughter conscious? When can we see Kate?"

"Due to the high fever, your granddaughter is in and out of consciousness. I'm sorry, Mrs. Breckenridge. No one will be allowed to see her until she's been admitted to a room." Dr. Patel shook Jack's hand. "I'm sorry you had to wait so long, but we had to get Mrs. Dolan stabilized first so we could run the necessary tests. We've also been swamped with trauma victims from a five-car collision." She turned to Kate's grandmother. "Dr. Jernigan shared with me a little of her medical history."

Martha Alice nodded. "The leukemia."

Dr. Patel tucked a loose tendril of black hair into the tight bun at the nape of her neck. "Kate's white platelet count is extremely low."

Martha Alice winced. "All these years, we've prayed the cancer would never return."

Dr. Patel's brown eyes were kind. "We will explore every treatment option. Can you tell me more about the age of onset and when she went into remission?"

Martha Alice went into a concise description of Kate's path to wellness as a child. "I'm so thankful she's come home from Africa." Her blue-veined hand touched the collar of her pale green blouse. "So she can receive the best-quality care."

Dr. Patel did a double take. "She's just returned from Africa?"

Martha Alice bit her lip. "Not quite two weeks ago."

"Sub-Saharan Africa?"

Jack looked from Russell Jernigan to the slender Indian doctor. "Best I recollect where the clinic was located, yes. Is that significant?"

The pediatrician looked as bewildered as he felt.

"It could be." Dr. Patel turned on her heel. "You will excuse me, please. There's something I must check." Punching numbers into the device on the wall, she flung open the door and ran back into triage.

CoraFaye planted her hands on her hips. "What was that about Africa, Russell?"

"I don't know, but I'll try to find out. Hang in there." Dr. Jernigan spoke to the lady at the information desk. She buzzed him through.

The automatic doors swished closed behind him. But not before Jack glimpsed a frenzy of activity on the other side.

And then someone on the hospital intercom called a Code Blue.

Chapter Thirteen

At the Code Blue alert, the color drained from Martha Alice's face. Jack helped her into a chair and feared she might soon require a Code Blue herself. Over the next agonizing hour, they waited for news.

Unable to focus, his mind ricocheted from one memory of Kate to another. He wore a path between the doors to triage and the waiting area.

"Sit down." Bridger caught his shirtsleeve. "You're making the other families antsy. Me, too."

"I—I can't." He ran his hand over his head. "I should be doing something to help her. I need to see her. I need to tell her I love her."

"When's the last time you told her?"

Jack scoured his face with his hand. "Today. This afternoon. Before she collapsed."

Had it only been a few hours since he'd pleaded with her to give them a second chance? It felt like days. A lifetime.

Bridger tightened his grip on Jack's shoulder. "Then she knows how you feel about her."

How he'd never stopped feeling about her.

"What if I never get to—"

"Don't go there." Bridger pulled him behind one of the decorative stone posts. "Now is the time to pray through the storm. And we're all in this with you."

He prayed with all his might and then some.

"Jack?"

At the sound of Russell Jernigan's voice, he opened his eyes.

"Dr. Patel has news she'd like to share with the family."

Stomach tanking, he scanned the pediatrician's face for any indication of what the news might be—good or bad. The Truelove doctor looked as tired as Jack felt. Bone-weary.

"Thank you for everything you've done." He touched the doctor's arm. "This would've been so much harder without you to pave the way."

Russell Jernigan gestured to the group waiting with Dr. Patel. "Come on, son." Except for the Truelove contingent, the waiting room had emptied of most of its other occupants.

Dr. Patel motioned to an empty set of chairs off to the side. "Perhaps it would be better if we sat over there to talk."

Martha Alice looked done in. Sitting on either side, his grandma and ErmaJean gripped her hands.

He knelt by the old woman. "If it's all the same to you, Miss Marth'Alice, I don't mind staying right where we are."

She nodded. "With the support of our friends."

Bracing for a blow, he held on to Martha Alice's hand. "Has Kate died, Dr. Patel?"

The Indian physician's dark eyes widened. "No, not at all. I didn't mean to frighten you. I have good news to report."

Martha Alice sucked in a breath. "Oh, Jack!"

Spots swam before his eyes. ErmaJean urged him into her vacated seat. Bridger pulled another chair for Dr. Patel.

"Kate's cancer has not returned. She is suffering from a disease that can mimic the symptoms of blood cancer." Dr. Patel leaned forward. "If all these years she's been subconsciously afraid of its return, I can understand her jumping to the wrong conclusion."

Jack's heart skipped a beat. "It isn't cancer?"

"It's a tropical disease called ehrlichiosis. A tick-borne disease more commonly known as African tick fever."

"A tick?" He frowned. "Like Rocky Mountain spotted fever?"

"Similar." The doctor nodded. "With many of the same symptoms as Lyme disease also, but endemic to parts of Africa and the French West Indies. The native population has a built-up, natural immunity. We most often see cases involving international travelers." She smiled at Martha Alice. "When you mentioned she'd only recently returned from Africa, it got me thinking of a case I treated when I did my residency in Miami. The patient was a man who'd spent time in Guadalupe. It's rare to encounter this disease in the United States."

Yet in the middle of the Blue Ridge Mountains, God had placed a doctor with the exact knowledge and expertise needed to help Kate.

"Is tick fever treatable?"

"Once I suspected she'd been bitten, I put her on doxycycline immediately. It's easily treated thanks to antibiotics." The doctor smiled. "She's already responding well. Her fever is going down. She's feeling better, awake and alert. I see no reason why she shouldn't make a full recovery."

Weak with relief, he slumped in the chair. CoraFaye choked back a sob. Subdued exclamations of joy broke out from among their Truelove friends. His aunt Georgie, Miss ErmaJean and Miss IdaLee swiped at their cheeks.

"Thank you, Lord." Martha Alice put a hand to her heart. "What about long-term complications?"

"I've had a chance to talk with Kate. She first noticed symptoms of a moderate headache, swollen lymph nodes and a low-grade fever the day before she left Africa. She has no recollection of a tick bite, but her team had been doing a field clinic in a remote section of the bush for several weeks. Left untreated, her condition worsened to a severe headache, joint pain, nausea and a debilitating fatigue."

"She tried to hide how unwell she felt." Martha Alice's mouth pursed. "I begged her to see a doctor. But she wouldn't hear of it."

Dr. Patel gave the older woman a rueful smile. "We medical professionals can be the worst about taking care of ourselves. Tick fever is rarely fatal, but if she'd left it much longer there could have been life-threatening complications leading to organ failure and death, especially for someone with a compromised immune system."

"I'm going to give that girl of mine a talking-to for scaring us." Martha Alice's eyes watered. "After I hug her first, of course." She took hold of the doctor's hands. "Thank you, Dr. Patel, for helping our stubborn, beautiful Kate."

The Indian woman patted her hand. "I'm glad I was able to help her."

Jack cleared his throat. "Can we see her now?"

Dr. Patel rose, and he rose with her. "We've moved her into a room. I think she'd love company." The doctor cut her eyes at the crowd surrounding them. "Because of her history, I'd like to keep her in the hospital for several days as a precaution. Also to give the antibiotic time to work." She stuck her hands in her lab coat pockets. "I can take you now, if you're ready."

Jack was more than ready. There was a flurry of quick hugs and goodbyes.

His grandmother touched his cheek. "Bring her home, Jack."

Jack reared a fraction. "Who are you, and what have you done with CoraFaye Dolan?"

"Stop being cheeky." His grandmother arched an eyebrow. "It's a bad wind that never changes." She touched his chin. "Don't forget to take care of yourself, too."

"I love you, Grandma."

Her blue eyes shone. "I love you back."

Bridger promised someone would drive Jack's truck to Asheville so he and Martha Alice would have transportation home when they needed it.

Dr. Patel led Jack and Martha Alice through the double doors and a maze of hallways to the elevator and up to the third floor. The doctor ushered them into Kate's room. "There are some people anxious to see your smiling face, Mrs. Dolan."

At the sight of Kate lying against the pale sheets, his heart caught in his throat. Martha Alice rushed forward. "Honey!"

Kate opened her arms as her grandmother rushed into them. Kate squeezed her eyes shut, but a single tear trekked its way down her cheek.

Dr. Patel turned to the door. "I'll leave you to your reunion."

After their last conversation, he wasn't sure if Kate wanted to see him. He studied her face as if he might never get the chance again. A possibility that had come far too close to becoming a reality.

She looked utterly spent, but her eyes were less glassy. Unlike the fiery spots of fever that dotted her cheeks before, a healthy color had returned to her features.

Kate released her grandmother. Her gaze found his and held. "Jack."

"You're a sight for sore eyes." His voice had become a husky thread.

The faint glimmer of a smile curved her lips. "I have a feeling I'm a sight sure enough." She smoothed her hand over her head.

Outside of Liddy, she was the most beautiful sight he'd ever beheld. And she always would be. The trauma of the past few hours hit him like a ton of bricks right between the eyes.

"I'll be back," he grunted.

He stumbled into the corridor. At the nurses' station, Dr. Patel took one look at him and hauled him into a vacant wheelchair parked next to the wall.

"I'm fine," he protested. The little woman was stronger than she looked. "I'm okay."

She pushed him down the hall. "I'll be the judge of that."

"I just needed some air."

Coming to the end of the corridor, she bumped a door open with her shoulder. Rolling him across the threshold, she brought him into a small chapel.

"It's always the biggest ones who fall the hardest. Give yourself a minute. Doctor's orders." The door swung shut behind her.

The enormity of almost losing Kate hit him hard. Getting out of the chair, he fell onto a nearby bench and dropped his head in his hands. But as long as there was life, there was hope for a second chance with Kate. *Thank You, God.*

After a brief time, he pulled himself together. Outside her room, he knocked.

"Come in," she called.

Feeling foolish, he shuffled inside.

Propped up in the hospital bed, her brow wrinkled. "Are you all right?"

"Fine." And he meant it this time. "I'm just glad you're not dying."

"Me, too." Her laugh was a shadow of the Kate he'd loved his entire life. But it was a laugh all the same. The first of more to follow. The beginning of the brighter tomorrow he prayed for.

Her lips quirked. "Reports of my death have been greatly exaggerated, Cowboy."

Cocking his head, he touched a finger to push up the brim of an imaginary Stetson. "I'm greatly relieved those reports were false."

Seated on a recliner next to the bed, Martha Alice looked from her granddaughter to Jack. She stood up. "I'm going to the cafeteria for a cup of tea."

He touched her arm. "I'll get that for you, Miss Marth'Alice."

"I want to stretch my legs." The older woman fluttered her hand. "Keep Kate company while I'm gone." Smiling, she left them.

Kate leaned against the pillow. "I'm glad you're here."

"I'm glad we're both here."

"About earlier..." Her mouth trembled. "Forgive me. I didn't mean what I said to you about Liddy's death."

"I know." He twined his fingers into hers. "We'll talk more once you feel stronger."

Closing her eyes, she drifted into a light slumber.

Forty minutes later, he was still holding her hand when Martha Alice returned. Dr. Patel gave him permission to stay with Kate overnight. He offered to drive Martha Alice home, but she refused.

"I'm not leaving my girl, either."

He gave Martha Alice the recliner, and he dozed upright in a straight-backed chair. Not a big deal. Over the course of his naval career, he'd slept in far worse conditions.

Within twenty-four hours, Kate's fever was gone. Over the next few days, she slowly regained her strength. There was a steady stream of Truelove well-wishers, bringing cards, balloons and flowers. Dr. Patel made tentative plans to discharge Kate later that weekend.

When Luke Morgan and his mom, Emily Jernigan, visited the hospital, Jack finally convinced Martha Alice to go home with them.

"I'll man the Kate fort," he assured her. "And make sure she doesn't exasperate the poor nurses assigned to her care."

"Right here." Kate waved her hand. "No need to talk about me as if I'm in the other room." She rolled her eyes.

That's when he knew for sure she was on the mend.

He urged Martha Alice to take a break. "Go home. Get a real shower, change your clothes and fix your hair."

"My hair?" Her eyes cutting to Emily, Martha Alice ran her hand over her gray locks. "Maybe Glenda at Hair Raisers would give me an emergency appointment."

"I think she might." Taking her elbow, Emily steered Martha Alice toward the door. "We'll give her a call from Luke's truck."

For the first time in several days, Jack found himself alone with Kate. For the zillionth time, he told her how thankful he was she was better. She asked about his progress on the house.

Hope surged in his heart. Was she envisioning herself there? Did she see a future with him?

With that wisp of encouragement, he barreled forward, in a rush to tell her how well things were going with the house and how she could be a part of it.

"The inspector's coming Friday." He grinned. "Then I'll get the certificate of occupancy. Just in time before you're released for good behavior into the world again."

Her gaze wavered. "About that…" She pleated the sheet with her fingers.

"Now that you've got a brand-new lease on life, we need to finalize our plans for the future."

Her smile faded. "Jack—"

"I love you, Kate. And you love me." He gripped her hand. "I can't wait for us to be together again. The way it was meant to be."

She jerked her hand free. "I'm not ready to be your wife, Jack. I'm not sure I'll ever be. I'm not even sure I want to stay in Truelove."

"We'll make it work this time, Kate." The intensity of his need to convince her overwhelmed him. To make her see sense. To prevent her from leaving again. "We're older and wiser. Our foundation isn't only about feelings, but grounded in commitment."

"Don't you see, Jack? There's no blueprint to fix what's really wrong with us. To fix what's wrong with me." She touched her chest. "I'll hurt you again. Worse this time than before. I'm no good for you. We're no good for each other. It's time we admitted that, and let each other go."

He'd not seen this coming.

"I don't believe that. Once again, you underestimate God. And you forget who I am." Frustration filled his voice. "Giving up isn't in my vocabulary. Navy SEALs don't quit. We don't quit in anticipation of future failure. Stop self-eliminating. I haven't quit on you. I haven't quit on us. And I don't intend to, Kate Dolan. Ever."

Kate's eyes glistened with tears. "I can't be the girl you fell in love with, Jack. That's who you miss. Who I was. Not who I am."

He rose. "I'll always love that summertime girl, but I don't believe she's entirely gone. I've seen sparks of her over the last two weeks. And I've already fallen in love with the brave woman you've become. A woman who's faced life's toughest storm and come out on the other side. The woman who brought health care to remote African villages. The woman who helped AnnaBeth and her baby."

"You're wrong. I'm not brave." Tears rolled down her cheeks. "I'm not brave enough to risk being with you again. I wouldn't survive failing this time. Failing you."

"Who says we'd fail?" She made him so crazy. "But thanks to Dr. Patel, you've got time to make up your mind what you want to do with the rest of your life. Here's a thought—" he yanked open the door to the hall "—instead of assuming we'd fail, why don't you think on how we'd succeed?"

He staggered into the corridor. Why must she be so stubborn? Blindsided by her obstinate refusal to give her life a second chance, he sagged against the wall. His anger swiftly gave way to despair, though, and the desperate fear he'd already lost her.

They'd both come so far, not only in terms of geographical distance. It couldn't end like this between them, could it? *Please, God, not again.*

The next day, Kate was released. She hadn't seen or heard from Jack since his angry exit. Beneath the anger, she knew she'd hurt him once more. Deeply.

She longed to comfort him. To hold him in her arms. To ease his sadness—a sadness she'd caused. But she'd thrown the privilege to mean anything in his life back in his face.

Faith had never come easy for Kate. Why did she have such a hard time trusting in a future with Jack? What lay at the heart of her hesitancy?

Once Dr. Patel signed the release order, Gram arrived to take her to Truelove. Per hospital policy, an orderly wheeled her to the exit.

"Simpler to walk," she muttered.

Following behind, her grandmother carried a bouquet of flowers. "Medical people make the worst patients."

The orderly parked Kate on the sidewalk. "I'll wait till your grandmother brings around the car."

"I believe our transportation has arrived." Gram fluttered her fingers at the driver behind the wheel of an all-too-familiar charcoal black GMC pickup.

Kate groaned. "I thought *you* were taking me home to Truelove."

Her grandmother smiled. "I love hearing you call Truelove home, but you know I don't drive in big-city traffic."

"It's Asheville, Gram. Not New York City."

The truck door dinged. Jack got out. The orderly gave him Kate's small duffel.

"Why didn't you tell me I'd be seeing Jack?" she hissed.

Gram sniffed. "The way you've been treating him, I didn't think you'd care if he saw you—" her grandmother flicked a look at her hair "—with hospital bed head."

"I've got bed—?" Sucking in a breath, she made a frantic effort to finger comb her hair into some semblance of order.

The orderly took the flower arrangement from her grandmother.

With Jack's assistance, Gram stepped into the cab.

Kate frantically tried to recall if she'd brushed her teeth before being discharged. She'd just come to the conclusion she had, when her gaze landed on a pair of scuffed, well-worn cowboy boots.

A mounting flush crept up her neck.

Hands on his hips, Jack smiled. "You can ride shotgun."

Did he always have to be so stinking attractive?

On the drive to Truelove, Jack and her grandmother kept up a steady conversation regarding various friends. Kate was afraid he was going to push her for information about her immediate plans, but he didn't.

She assumed he didn't because of Gram. Until they neared the outskirts of Truelove, he didn't talk to her at all.

Throwing her the devastating smile, which never failed to create goose bumps on her skin, he cut his eyes at her. "Almost home now."

An image of the white board-and-batten farmhouse with dormers and black-framed windows popped into her mind.

But he pulled into the Breckenridge driveway, and she fought against a ridiculous sense of disappointment. Not the "almost home" she'd envisioned. The farmhouse couldn't be her home. It was Jack's.

After helping Gram transition her into the house, he bid them farewell and left. She stared out the window long after the taillights disappeared down the street.

He'd been kind, considerate and cordial. There'd been absolutely no pressure on her to choose to stay. She had nothing to reproach him for and yet here she was. A growing sense of dissatisfaction at the way they'd left things made mincemeat of her stomach.

She reassured herself he'd return tomorrow, and they'd talk then. But he didn't come over with Gram after church. Nor did he visit the next day, either. She waited all day, jumping every time the phone rang.

Gram turned off the kitchen faucet. "I'm too old for this foolishness. If you want to talk to him, call him yourself. You love him. Put the man out of his misery."

Kate plopped on the sofa and hugged a cushion. "We loved each other before and look how well that didn't turn out."

Her grandmother set the metal watering can with a clang onto the counter. Marching around the island, she stalked into the living room. Kate hadn't seen her move that fast since… Since high school when Kate stayed out too late one night.

With Jack, of course.

"Aren't you tired of using the same old excuse?" Perched on the edge of the armchair, Gram folded her hands in her lap, her ankles tucked next to the chair. "Because I'm tired of hearing it."

Kate blinked. "Excuse me?"

"No, I won't. Not any longer." This was the Martha Alice librarian voice reserved for malefactors who dared mistreat one of her precious books. "I've been kind. I've been patient. I've made excuses to the whole town. I can't see it's done you any good. First, you couldn't be with Jack because of Liddy. Then, you couldn't be with him because you were supposedly dying."

"You don't understand what I've been through." Glaring, she clutched the pillow to her chest. "I lost my child."

"Stop punishing him. Stop punishing yourself."

"I'm not."

Gram poked her in the side. "Stop slouching when I'm talking to you, Katie Rose."

"Ow!" But her spine instantly straightened.

"Would you handle Liddy's death the same way today?"

Kate shook her head. "No."

"What would you do differently?"

She gnawed at her lip. "I wouldn't run away. I'd stay and face the pain. I'd face Jack's pain and maybe we could help each other."

"You've both learned from your mistakes. What makes you think if adversity visited you again that you'd fail each other? Or maybe you don't really love Jack at all."

"That's not true." Kate scowled. "I do love Jack. Love is the easy part."

Her grandmother gave her a cool look. "You're right. Love from afar is easy. It takes courage to build a life and a family together. To persevere is hard."

"You think Jack and I should get back together?"

"I never believed you should've left him in the first place." Gram touched her cheek. "Don't let the fear win this time. You of all people understand how fragile life truly is. But life is precious. It must be cherished. And love—real love—is worth fighting for, my dear."

Kate blinked away her tears, unable to trust herself to speak.

Gram hugged her. "I'm going to putter in my garden where I do my best praying. I won't bother asking you to listen for the phone." Her grandmother smirked. "Because I know you'll do that anyway."

"Sarcasm is unbecoming in a woman of your maturity, Gram."

Her grandmother pursed her lips. "So is self-pity in a woman of yours."

Ouch.

It was nearly bedtime when Jack called. "How was your day?"

"Good." It had been a terrible day. She'd been a bundle of nerves. "How about you?"

"Busy."

That was his only explanation for not hearing from him?

Kate was aware she was being irrational and unreasonable. "I—I thought I might see you by now."

There was a beat of silence.

Perhaps she'd pushed him away one time too many. CoraFaye was right about her. Who wanted a psychoneedy person like her in their lives?

He cleared his throat. "I wanted to let you get settled."

"I'm settled."

She winced at the little-girl-lost quality to her voice. He'd finally wised up and decided to run as far away from her as possible. She didn't blame him. She—

"Do you trust me, Kate?"

Trust. Respect. Love. All of the above.

She felt a rush of tenderness. "I trust you, Jack."

"I've been putting together something for you. For both of us. A long time in the making. I was waiting on a call to confirm the details. Are you up for a road trip to Asheville in a couple of days?"

Her brows drew together. "What's going on?"

"I'd rather not say."

Why was he being so mysterious? "Something fun?"

"Not really." He sighed. "But something helpful. I hope."

She blew out a breath. "I won't see you until then?"

"It's only a couple of days."

She squeezed her eyes shut. "It's just I miss you," she whispered into the phone.

He chuckled the throaty laugh that turned her insides into mush. "I miss you, too." Whatever tension there'd existed between them, either real or imagined on her part, seemed to dissipate.

They spent another thirty minutes talking—really talking—about their day. The funny antics of a colt. How her pacing and waiting for Jack's call had Gram declaring Kate was getting on her last nerve.

"I didn't mean to call so late," he apologized. "The day got away from me. I did manage to put the last finishing touches on the house. It's move-in ready now."

Leaning her head to rest on the chair, she smiled. "Should I take that as a personal invitation?"

"Darlin', yours is a standing invitation."

His voice, husky with emotion, sent a tingle down to her toes. Part of her wanted to fling herself into the life he offered. No holds barred. Without reservation. But she didn't.

Jack didn't pressure her. He ended the call with only a hint of the disappointment he must feel. And she hated herself again for the umpteenth time.

She loved, loved, loved Jack Dolan. She had loved him her entire life. Love had never been the issue between them. If only life were that simple. But life—her life—wasn't that simple. If anything, she loved him too much to drag him down with her into the emotional quagmire of her existence.

Must it always be two steps forward, one step back with her and Jack? Why couldn't she move past her fear of a future with him?

What's wrong with me?

Chapter Fourteen

That night, Kate went to bed depleted and discouraged. *Thank You, God, she wasn't dying.* But nothing else had changed. She was still so adrift about what her future should look like.

However, busy was better than wallowing.

She spent the next few days consulting with Dr. Jernigan on a project dear to both their hearts—establishing a women's health center in Truelove so local women didn't have to travel over the mountain in often-iffy weather or long-distance to Asheville to receive the health care they needed.

After what happened to AnnaBeth and her granddaughter, Victoria Cummings, with her influential connections, also came onto the advisory board. And to Kate's everlasting surprise, so did CoraFaye.

They held their first organizational meeting at the Jar. It was CoraFaye's brilliant idea to purchase a block of abandoned storefront near Dr. Jernigan's pediatric office.

"It's been empty since the highway bypassed Truelove. GeorgeAnne's family have owned that stretch of real estate for eons. She'd sell it for a song to a worthy business, bringing life back to our downtown. Plus, there's a parking lot behind it." CoraFaye pushed her eyeglasses higher on the bridge of her nose. "The biggest expense would be the renovation into a clinic."

The fledging board voted to purchase the property. When Kate left the diner, Victoria was already messaging deep-pocketed friends.

On Thursday, Kate made the trip with Jack to Asheville. When he pulled into the hospital, she threw him an anxious glance. "Why are we here?"

Parking, he cut the engine. "You don't have to come if you don't want to, but I am going to meet her."

Kate's heart ticked up a notch. "Who?"

He gripped the steering wheel. "In the midst of shock and grief, we made the decision to donate Liddy's organs."

Kate's stomach knotted.

"Seven lives were transformed because of our decision. They are Liddy's truest legacy, Kate." His eyes beseeched her to understand. "From the first, I wanted to know who they were, what was their story. Then you left and I... I..." He strangled the wheel.

Her lungs constricted.

"Recipients and donor families don't always meet. But one recipient's mom wrote a letter to the organ procurement organization to thank us for our sacrifice."

She fought the urge to curl into a ball.

He faced her. "For the last two years, we've corresponded. We exchanged phone numbers. Phoebe called me the day you were released from the hospital. I can't help but see God's hand in this. They're on the way from their home in Raleigh to a family vacation in Gatlinburg."

She put her hand to her throat.

"Owen and Phoebe—they're her parents—we've been wanting to meet for ages. Since she was old enough to understand the gift we'd given her, Ivy has wanted to thank us in person. The OPO thought it might be best if we met in a neutral setting. They've arranged for a small reception room to be available."

Kate swallowed hard. "Ivy."

"I told Phoebe I wasn't sure you'd agree. I'm still not sure, but I told her I would try." He took her hand. "I will never force you to do anything you don't feel ready for. It's your choice. Your decision."

She looked at him. This was important to him. Perhaps even necessary in healing the hole Liddy's loss had left in his heart. Probably just as essential for her, too. But he wouldn't push. He wouldn't insist.

Tears sprang into her eyes. "You are the best man I've ever known, Jack Dolan."

His hand went to her cheek. "Kate…" The longing, the yearning in his voice, for her—and her well-being— shattered something coiled tight inside her for too long.

With a cold, crystal clarity, she beheld the true source of her problem. It was herself she didn't trust. Nor the goodness of God.

She'd never doubted His ability to do the impossible. Her real issue was faith in His willingness to act for her good.

Gram was right. She couldn't go on like this. In that moment, she relinquished her futile attempts to control a future no one but God could foresee. *Help me to trust You.*

No matter what the future might hold, she gave herself and Jack into His hands.

"Tell me about Ivy." Turning her face into his hand, she kissed his palm. "Prepare me for what I'm walking into. Help me." She bit her lip.

"Always, my darlin'. Always."

Over the next few minutes, he laid out the facts as he understood them.

"Ivy is five years old."

"Like—" Kate's voice broke.

He held her hands in his. "Same age as Liddy would've been."

At six months old, the little girl was diagnosed with an enlarged heart and severe heart failure.

"By the time she was eighteen months old, something called a Berlin heart—"

"A ventricular device to keep her blood flowing. Only used for end-stage heart failure."

He smiled, but there was a sadness in his eyes. "I'm not surprised Nurse Kate knows about it."

She took a breath. "The longest any patient has survived on the device is 192 days."

"Ivy needed a transplant to save her life." He squeezed her fingers so hard she winced. "The call came—Liddy died—on Ivy's one hundred and ninety-first day, Kate."

God's sometimes unfathomable, always beautiful timing.

A sob caught in her throat. She wasn't sure she could walk into the hospital and meet the child whose life would go on. While Liddy's wouldn't.

Trust, Kate. The threaded whisper floated across her mind. Gentle and loving. Like Jack.

She let go of his hands and swiped the tears from her face. "Let's do this before I lose my nerve."

"Thank you, Kate. Thank you for not making me do this alone. You are the strongest woman I've ever known."

She reached for the door handle. "I'm not strong." She was broken and so weak. She understood now that any strength she'd ever possessed was from God.

The entrance doors opened, then closed behind them.

He guided her along several long corridors until he found the correct room number. A slim woman in her late twenties rose from the chintz sofa. "Jack?"

"I'm Jack." He stepped forward. "Phoebe Upton?"

Tucking a strand of dark brown hair behind her ear, she nodded. "Hello."

"This is my…" He faltered. "This is Kate."

Praying not to fall apart, she held herself tight.

He glanced around the empty room. "Where's Owen and Ivy?"

"Owen took Ivy to see the fish aquarium outside the cafeteria to give us a few minutes."

Jack shook her hand. "I can't tell you what this means to meet your family, Phoebe. I'm so grateful."

For a second, Kate feared the woman might extend her hand to her as well. But if she did, Phoebe apparently reconsidered and dropped her hand. Kate wasn't sure she could bear to be touched.

"We're the ones who are grateful." Phoebe's brown eyes cut to Kate. "When the call came to the pediatric transplant ward at Duke, we felt such relief, excitement, hope…" Her full lips trembled. "Yet it was bittersweet because it meant somewhere there was another family dealing with such unimaginable pain. I can't begin to comprehend how you found the strength to make the hardest of decisions."

Organ donation hadn't been their hardest decision. Turning off the machine keeping Liddy's body functioning had been the hardest. An acknowledgment all hope of life was gone.

At least, life—as Kate was slowly learning—on this earth.

Kate reached for Jack, and he took her hand. Outside of God, he was her anchor, her lifeline.

She found her voice. "Jack and I were in immediate agreement. Part of Liddy would give someone else the chance to live and do the things she'd never get to do. We'd never want to take that from another family." She surprised herself by touching Phoebe's sleeve.

Phoebe blinked back tears. "Thank you for coming, Kate. Owen and I wanted the person who gave Ivy her new heart to be more than just a name to her."

Oh, God, help me.

Someone knocked. Phoebe opened the door to a man and a little girl.

Carrying what looked like poster board, Owen introduced himself, but Kate only had eyes for the dark-haired sprite dressed in an iridescent tutu with wings. Wearing a sparkly tiara, the child held a bouquet of flowers.

Phoebe stood behind her daughter. "Ivy insisted on wearing her butterfly princess costume to meet you today."

"What could be more appropriate than a butterfly princess?" Kate dropped to her knees to be closer to the child's level. "Hello, Ivy."

She was surprised at the steadiness in her voice.

Hugging her mother's leg, Ivy gave Kate a shy smile.

Phoebe put her hand on her daughter's hair. "This is Liddy's mom and dad."

Ivy held out the flowers to Kate.

Sunflowers. Liddy's favorite. Had Jack told them? She darted a look at him, but with a bemused smile, he shook his head slightly, sharing the wonder of it with her.

"These are beautiful." She smiled at the little girl. "Just like you."

Ivy pulled at her father. "Daddy?"

Owen handed his daughter the poster board. Covered with stars and stickers, it read, "Thank you."

Ivy passed it to Jack and held up three small fingers. "It's my third heart-versary."

Phoebe threw Kate an apologetic look. "They—they know that, honey."

All too well.

Owen motioned toward a stethoscope draped over the arm of the sofa. "Would you like to sit down? The OPO suggested you might want to listen to Ivy's... Liddy's..." He gulped.

Jack didn't respond. Glancing at him, Kate rose. Ivy's soft-spoken "Daddy" had proved his emotional undoing. Her handsome, rugged cowboy. Her tough Navy SEAL. It was her turn to be strong for him. For them both.

"We'd love to. Thank you." Gripping his hand, she guided him to the sofa. They sat on one end. Phoebe sat down on the other. Ivy slipped into her mother's lap.

Kate laid the flowers on the side table.

"Jack told us what a wonderful nurse-midwife you are." Owen handed Kate the stethoscope. "I'm guessing you're pretty familiar with how to use this. More so than us."

Kate fit the earpieces on Jack. She rubbed the bell, warming it with her palm. "Can we take a listen, Ivy?"

Smiling sweetly, the little girl nodded and leaned forward.

Kate placed the bell on Ivy's chest.

A muscle ticked in his jaw, but somehow Jack's eyes remained dry. "You have a good heart in there, Miss Ivy."

She giggled.

And it was Kate's turn to listen to Liddy's heart, beating inside Ivy.

Tears slid down her cheeks. The last time she'd listened to Liddy's heart had been in a faraway hospital in Virginia Beach right before she died.

Jack wrapped his arms around her.

Owen sat beside his wife. "In the darkest moment of your life, you chose to spare someone else that pain..." He choked up. "I can't begin to express how much your daughter's gift meant to us. To give a child you never knew another chance at life." His dark eyes so like Ivy's swam with tears. "It's—it's kind of overwhelming and beautiful and we're so thankful to you."

"I love Liddy so much." Ivy placed her small hand over Kate's, still holding the bell against the child's chest. "I 'member her birthday every year."

Her smile tore at Kate's heart.

"Thank you for remembering her, sweetheart."

"I not ever gonna forget." Ivy touched a finger and caught a silent tear on Kate's cheek. "We're best friends."

Just like that, one of a bereaved parent's worst fears—that her child would be forgotten—was laid to rest. God *was* good. So good.

Ivy sat back. "Can I listen to your heart, Miss Kate?"

She couldn't help but chuckle at the "Miss." Spoken like a properly raised Southern child.

"Of course you can." She transferred the ear tips to Ivy and positioned the bell on her own chest. "How does my heart sound, Ivy?"

"It sounds real good." Ivy's brown eyes shone. "My turn again. You listen to mine."

Kate obliged.

"What's my heart sound like, Miss Kate?"

Like golden blond curls. Silvery laughter. And happiness.

Sheer happiness.

"It's saying, lubba-dubba. Lubba-dubba, dear Ivy."

The little girl laughed with delight.

"Do you know what lubba-dubba means, Ivy?"

"What does it mean, Miss Kate?"

Closing her eyes, she pressed her forehead against Ivy's. The little girl smelled of baby shampoo.

"It means I lubba-dubba you," she whispered to the steady, soothing heartbeat of her child.

Kate held it together long enough for addresses to be exchanged. The Uptons promised to send photos of life's milestones. Like the first day of kindergarten, high school graduation, dancing at a someday wedding. And in between, getting together in person once in a while.

She and Jack made it to his truck before they collapsed into each other's arms. Thankful for a screen of hollies, she wept and clung to him—as he did to her—the way they should have done in the days following Liddy's death. And they talked about what they'd each felt that day.

When the hurricane of tears subsided, she felt something different. There'd been tears before—countless drops enough to fill an ocean. She didn't fool herself that in the years ahead, there wouldn't be more.

A parent never got over losing a child. The wound would always be there. But the unbearable agony was gone. This time, there'd been a healing in her tears. For Jack, too.

Each of them processing what they'd just experienced, they didn't talk much on the road to Truelove. As the ribbon of highway wound over the foothills of the Blue Ridge, her gaze roamed over the explosion of purple, white and pink rhododendrons blanketing the hillsides.

The drive gave her time to ponder what she wanted her future to hold. And what she didn't want it to hold. Thanks be to God, she had a future.

She cut her eyes to Jack. Turning his head, he smiled.

Her heart took flight. As it had the moment he first smiled at her those many years ago.

Was a future possible for them? *Just trust...* And she knew that it was.

Reconciliation and love lay at the core of God's heart for every man, woman and child. Love for her. For Jack. For the life they would rebuild together.

Not far from Truelove, she fluttered her hand toward the overlook, a view of the purplish-blue mountains. "I need you to pull over."

He tightened his grip on the wheel. "Are you okay?" Quickly, he brought the truck to a stop. "What's wrong?"

In the valley below, the silvery glint of the river, older than the mountains, curved around the sleepy little town like an embrace. A patchwork kingdom of green forests, yellow hay fields and apple orchards spread out before them. Somewhere not quite visible but just beyond lay the grassy, glorious bald of Dolan Mountain.

"Nothing's wrong. At least, I hope not. I hope it's the beginning of something right." She took a breath. "I'm staying in Truelove."

She told him about the plans for the new women's clinic. Dr. Jernigan had already offered her a job. His wife, Emily, was heading the search to staff the center with a receptionist, accounts manager, an OB-GYN with a passion for rural health care and a couple of labor and delivery nurse-midwives like Kate.

"What do you think about me staying?"

His eyes never left her face. "I think you should do what you think is best."

"I told you what I thought." She thumped his bicep. "I want to know what you think, Cowboy."

Smirking, he rubbed his arm. "I think you and Cora-Faye are exactly the—"

"If you finish that thought—" she wagged her finger "—I will not be responsible for what happens next."

"Welcome back, Kate." He grinned, still rubbing his arm. "I'd love for you to stay in Truelove." His smiled faded. "But what else do you want to be a part of your new life?"

The uncertainty in his eyes—the self-doubt she'd put there—slammed into her like a 4-by-4. *God, forgive me.* Jack, too. She had so much damage to repair.

"I want time with Gram."

He nodded.

"I want a support system in my life."

Jack swallowed. "We all need that."

"I want to develop meaningful relationships with friends like AnnaBeth and Maggie."

"Good idea. Is that all?"

Not for the first time, she believed she might drown in the blueness of his eyes.

"Most of all—" she twined her fingers through his "—I want to spend the rest of my life loving you. I want a second chance to love you the way you deserve to be loved." She bit her lip. "If you'll have me."

"Darlin' Kate, I'm yours. I always have been." His eyes locked onto hers. "You had only to ask for me to be yours again. Forever."

"I love you so much, Jack."

She leaned across the seat, eager to feel his lips on hers. Cradling her face between his palms, his mouth brushed her lips, and it felt oh so right.

After a moment, he pulled back, but held her close in the circle of his arms. "I'm not sure what happens next in situations like ours. Do I call the preacher? Do I take out a marriage license?"

She laughed. "Technically, we're still married." She

traced his jawline with her finger. "Although, I wouldn't be opposed to renewing our vows in the near future." She took a deep breath. "But right now, I only want to go home to where we'll build a new life together."

Once more, they headed toward Truelove, where true love awaited. Toward a future, wrought from the pain of the past. Broken, but restored, the light of their love shone through the cracks of their lives. Shining all the more because of the cracks. Because of God's love for her and Jack.

Love made everything possible.

Chapter Fifteen

Two Years Later—Autumn

"Done for the day?"

Kate glanced at the young doctor in scrubs. "Last patient seen." She pushed her office chair away from the desk. "Final medical chart updated until Monday. How about you?"

"Definitely ready for the weekend."

He was a recent hire, lured straight out of residency. Dr. Jernigan had been as good as his word about helping Kate open a women's health clinic down the street from his pediatric practice. AnnaBeth's fundraising genius of a mom, Victoria, had also been crucial in making this dream a reality.

"Per Miss Marth'Alice's suggestion—" He looked at Kate to make sure he was saying it "right."

She smiled at his fervor to fit in.

The young OB-GYN folded his arms. "I'm driving to the Parkway to see the leaves." He flushed. "Which makes me just another newbie leaf-peeper, I guess."

Hailing from tropical Florida, this was his first leaf-change, the kind of spectacle for which the Blue Ridge was famous. His endearing eagerness to belong had won the collective hearts of Truelove's young and old.

She retrieved her purse from a drawer. "Nothing wrong with being a leaf-peeper. It's gorgeous this time of year."

He had the makings of an excellent physician. Smart but, more importantly, he had a heart for his patients and a passion for rural health care. He'd already proved a godsend to the fledging Truelove Women's Health Center.

She slung the purse strap over her shoulder. "Don't forget to stop by Apple Valley Orchard to get hot cider and the best apple doughnuts you'll ever eat. Tell Callie and Jake hello from me."

The doctor grinned. "Looking forward to it. You've got an important afternoon ahead of you."

She was only working a half day so she'd have some time before the meeting.

"Are you nervous?"

She'd been up-front about her personal struggles. "A little." She lifted her chin. "But ready for this next chapter."

Kate had worked hard over the last few years to make new dreams for herself with Jack. Ever and always with Jack.

Hands dug deep in the pockets of his white coat, he followed her to the reception area. "I'll keep you in my prayers."

"I appreciate that more than you know."

Such a nice young man. She waved goodbye to their receptionist.

He held open the door for Kate. "Miss IdaLee told me to stop by her house before I leave tomorrow morning.

She's packed a picnic for when I'm on the Parkway. I can't get over how friendly everybody is here."

That was certainly one way to look at it.

Kate bit her lip to keep from laughing. Little did he know his bachelor days were numbered. With his boy-next-door good looks and baby-face demeanor, he'd become the matchmakers' current matrimonial project. He didn't stand a chance against the combined machinations of Truelove's most lovable citizens.

She had it on good authority from Gram that one of Miss IdaLee's ubiquitous nieces was also in town. Kate had a feeling the picnic was for two, and the socially shy young doctor wouldn't be taking in the leaf-color alone.

God bless him. And the dear ladies with their proclivity for happily-ever-after mayhem. After all, they hadn't done so badly when it came to her and Jack.

She patted his arm. "Just remember, resistance is futile."

He blinked at her. "What?"

"Never mind. Have fun."

She left him at the door, staring after her.

In the parking lot, Maggie waited beside Kate's car. "Supper from the Jar." Looking radiant, she hefted a white paper bag. "So you won't have to worry about cooking dinner tonight."

She and Maggie had become close. Soon, the recreational director would become her latest midwife client. After telling their families, Kate had been the first one with whom Maggie shared her momentous news. She was thrilled for Maggie and Bridger.

"Kara insisted on throwing in enough to feed a tiny army. You know how she loves to feed people. There's a whole tub of the fancy French mac 'n cheese Jack adores."

Maggie grinned. "Also included, Austin has sent a drawing. And Logan is sharing a favorite book."

After the trauma Maggie endured with the birth of the twins, her dear friend never expected to want to go through another pregnancy. But facing their fears together, she and Bridger had made the decision to have another child.

Maggie wasn't the only one finding the courage to do a new thing. Though Kate and Jack had made a different sort of decision.

"I'm so scared, Mags." Her lips trembled. "What if I fail *him*?"

"You won't." Maggie cocked her head. "Have you changed your mind?"

She blew out a breath. "I haven't. I want to do this. Really."

Maggie gave her a slow nod. "It's nerves, then. And to be expected. But you'll be all right."

Clicking her key fob, Kate loaded the food into the back seat. "You headed to the rec center next?"

"For a little while. Then carpool."

Kate leaned against the car door. "I can't believe the twins are already in second grade."

A bittersweet milestone. If she'd lived, so too would Liddy.

"Me, either." Reaching behind her head, Maggie tightened her ponytail. "Swim lessons are ending this week. I'll email you this quarter's financials."

Over the last two years, Jack and Kate had visited Ivy and her parents several times. Raleigh wasn't that far. Jack had been right about Ivy and the other organ recipients being Liddy's greatest legacy. She and Jack had thought a lot about what else they wanted her legacy to be. Dreaming of what her legacy could yet become.

They'd created the Lydia Mae Dolan Scholarship. Per Maggie's leadership, the fund provided free swim lessons for children whose parents couldn't afford them.

Maggie hopped into her truck, closed the door and leaned through the open window. "Call me when you get the chance. I'll be praying."

Kate got into her car. "Thanks." She waved goodbye.

Her car rattled over the bridge as she headed out of town. She forced her left knee to stop jiggling. *Yep.* She was definitely fighting nerves.

She smiled at the *Welcome to Truelove* sign. True love had certainly awaited her and Jack. A week after meeting Ivy, she and Jack renewed their vows in the meadow beside the house Jack built for her. It had been a busy but very happy two years as she and Jack rebuilt their lives together. A life based on the One Who loved them first and the most.

The ridge was a riot of orange, red and yellow leaves.

Grief was a lifelong journey. Like hiking Dolan Mountain, she carried the weight of her grief like a backpack she'd never completely lay aside.

But over time, the agonizing pain had softened. The pack had grown lighter and she found she could enjoy life again. Forever changed by Liddy's death, it was impossible for her and Jack to be the people they once were, but they were no longer forever sad.

Saving other families from experiencing the grief she and Jack endured had become a worthwhile endeavor to Liddy's memory. There wasn't a single day she didn't miss Liddy or ache to hold her in her arms. And she always would.

But the good days far outweighed the bad. It made her smile to think how proud Liddy would be of her mom and dad.

"We're trying, baby," she whispered. "We're trying."

She turned into the ranch. Glimpsing Victoria's luxury SUV parked between the barn and the farmhouse—distinctive in a region where most vehicles were trucks—she couldn't resist the urge to stop and say hello.

And she was also desperate to distract herself from the all-important meeting this afternoon.

Since she returned to Truelove, one of the more inexplicable happenings had been the friendship between AnnaBeth's elegant, society mother, Victoria, and Jack's often irascible, always-in-your-face grandmother, Cora-Faye.

Victoria maintained CoraFaye had saved her daughter and granddaughter's lives. CoraFaye was just plain bewildered someone like Victoria wanted to be her friend. CoraFaye was older by a number of years, but they were more alike than they were different. Small, feisty women. Tornado and hurricane. Forces of nature.

CoraFaye taught Victoria how to clean out horse stalls. Victoria got CoraFaye to leave the ranch for a mani-pedi in Charlotte. Currently, fashionista Victoria had decided it was her mission in life to give CoraFaye a makeover.

God bless her.

CoraFaye sat in the middle of the screened porch in a straight-backed kitchen chair. Victoria stood behind her, fussing with CoraFaye's long, salt-and-pepper braid.

Victoria looked up and smiled. "Hey, sugar pie."

CoraFaye glowered. "Kate."

By now, she understood Jack's grandmother didn't mean anything by it. The older woman's face just didn't do happy. They both loved Jack, and that was all that really mattered.

She and CoraFaye had made their peace with each other. In a weird, never-thought-it-would-happen way, she'd come to value CoraFaye's give-it-to-me-straight perspective on life. She'd always know where she stood with the older woman.

Kate hated to admit it, but Jack was right. In many ways, she and CoraFaye were very alike. Those they loved, they loved fiercely and forever.

She raised her eyebrow. "What are you two up to now?"

"Nothing good," his grandmother growled.

Victoria gestured at CoraFaye's face. "Will you look at those cheekbones? They're practically begging for a touch of pink."

CoraFaye snorted.

Victoria rummaged through a makeup bag on a nearby stool. "Where's my bronzer?"

CoraFaye rolled her eyes. "Why I put up with your foolishness I don't know."

Victoria emerged triumphant, makeup brush in hand. "When I get through with C-F, you won't recognize her."

CoraFaye scowled. "Tori, I done told you…"

Kate knew better than to smile. The two besties had nicknames for each other. So cute. She was glad his grandmother's life had become so full.

"Just joking." Victoria shot Kate a slightly wicked grin. "Actually, C-F's style is more casual and natural." She mentioned a particular supermodel.

CoraFaye threw Kate a look of horror. "Save me," she whispered.

She laughed. "Why are you letting her do this?" Cora-Faye never did anything she didn't want to do.

The older woman shrugged her skinny shoulders. "A little paint never hurt an old barn." She blushed a becoming shade of pink. "Don't want to scare the little guy first glance."

At the sudden reminder, Kate swallowed convulsively.

Jack's grandmother bounded out of the chair. "I made cinnamon buns for your breakfast tomorrow."

CoraFaye's cinnamon buns were not to be turned down.

She and Victoria followed Jack's grandmother into the kitchen. "Thank you, Miss CoraFaye."

"It's going to be okay." CoraFaye's eyes misted. "I feel it in my heart." She gave Kate an awkward side hug, but a hug all the same.

Would wonders never cease? But Kate was grateful for how far they'd come. She hugged the older woman. Stiffening only slightly, CoraFaye patted Kate's back before quickly pulling away.

She thrust the plate of cinnamon buns at Kate. "See that you don't let Jack get to 'em before the boy, or there won't be any left."

"Yes, ma'am."

Behind the horn-rimmed eyeglasses, CoraFaye blinked rapidly. As if sensing her friend was about to lose it, Victoria slipped her arm around Kate's shoulders and walked her out of the kitchen to the screened porch.

Clutching the plate to her chest, her senses whirled. "How did you do it, Victoria?" she whispered. "How?"

AnnaBeth had admitted she hadn't made it easy on her stepmother all those years ago. But now, Kate had never met any mother and daughter—biological or otherwise—closer.

"They grow not under your heart—" Victoria cupped Kate's cheek "—but in it, dear one."

She retraced her steps to the car.

Beyond the bend and a grove of trees, she veered into the garage of the house Jack had built for her with its sweeping view of Dolan Mountain, awash in the color of a Blue Ridge autumn.

Jack was probably still at the barn. He'd be home soon. She put away the food. People in Truelove were kind. She changed out of her clinical scrubs into jeans and a gray sweater.

Sitting at the breakfast table, she was going through the emails on her tablet when the back door squeaked open and Jack appeared. The sight of him never failed to make her heart turn over.

Jack's eyes were warm with the look he reserved for her. "Hey, beautiful." He planted a sweet kiss on her forehead.

"Hey yourself, Cowboy."

Jack drifted to the sink. "What's up?"

"A few more invitations to speak." She scrolled. "From the mothers of a preschool group in a small town outside Greensboro. It's somebody Mags and Bridger know. Also, there's one from a PTA in Wilmington."

He rolled his shirtsleeves to his elbows and turned on the faucet. "We agreed to table the speaking engagements for a while." He soaped his ropey forearms.

Speaking wherever there were children and parents, she and Jack had become tireless advocates on how to keep children safer around the water. Thanks to Anna-Beth's connections, at the beginning of summer each year, they had a standing invitation to appear on a local Asheville television show to talk about what drowning looked like, how quickly it could happen and water safety tips.

It had come as no surprise to her the camera loved Jack. His quiet competence and undeniable charisma had connected with viewers. The cowboy swagger hadn't hurt, either.

Nor the oft-touted witty banter.

Smiling to herself, she positioned her fingers over the keyboard. "I'll decline."

"Hang on a minute." He grabbed a dish towel. "Bridger told me about that little town outside of Greensboro. Not too far from the zoo. As for the gig in Wilmington?" He dried his hands. "Great excuse to sneak in a trip to the beach. Maybe our first family vacation. Be fun, huh?"

"Fun." Anxiety gnawed at her insides. "Yeah."

"Aunt Georgie insists we bring him by the hardware store soon. She's got these little cowboy boots she wants to give him." He grinned. "Sweet of her."

Kate put her hands in her lap. "Very."

Trust...

Jack cut his eyes at the wall clock. "Not too much longer." He pulled her out of the chair and into an embrace. She savored the aroma of hay, leather and Jack.

He caught her chin between his thumb and forefinger, lifting her face to his. "What would you think of getting ice cream after seeing Aunt Georgie?" His eyes, filled with a tinge of uncertainty, locked onto hers.

On the surface, she might appear her usual, calm, collected professional self, but on the inside she was quaking at the enormity of what they were about to undertake. Unsure of herself, but sure of Jack. He wanted this so much. So very, very much.

And she loved Jack so very, very much.

Trust...

"Ice cream is a great idea," she rasped.

Outside, there was the sound of a car.

Her mouth went dry. She put her hand over her wildly beating heart. Was Jack as excited-scared-terrified as she was?

As usual, he read her so well. He twined his fingers through hers. "We got this, darlin'." His breath brushed the tendrils of hair dangling around her ears. "Even better, God's got us."

She and Jack had prayed so hard and so long over this next step in their journey. Overcome so many challenges. There'd been countless, deep conversations between them to make sure they were okay with each part of the process.

They'd taken classes. Had hours of counseling. Filled out a forest of application forms. Were interviewed by innumerable county officials. They searched and searched their hearts.

She and Jack headed toward the foyer. The doorbell buzzed. Her heart threatened to leap out of her chest.

He squeezed her hand, then let go. Opening the door, Jack greeted their guests. He stepped aside to allow the older woman and her small charge to come inside.

She'd had so many questions leading up to this moment. Each question, answered one by one. Except one last, burning question she couldn't yet shake.

Can I ever love another child like I love Liddy?

The caseworker brought the little boy forward. In his blue denim jacket and preschooler jeans, he was small for his age. Taken from an abusive home into the foster care system. Behind the brown frames and thick lenses, his face pinched with fear.

He huddled against the older woman. Life had already taught him he was unwanted. And unloved?

Trust... A single ray of sunshine illumined his brown hair. Her breath caught.

When his dark eyes locked onto hers, Kate had her answer. Victoria was right. Not under her heart. But in it.

Like the promise of spring, something sweet, pure and as beautiful as Liddy unfurled in her chest. This was her child. The son she was meant to have all along. And at last, they'd found each other.

Owen Upton's words from that first meeting in Asheville floated back to her about giving a child she'd never known another chance at life. Overwhelming and beautiful, he'd said. And it was, but she was also so thankful.

"Hello, Finn. I'm Kate." Dropping to her knees, she smiled at him, her heart in her eyes. "Welcome home, my darling."

* * * * *

Dear Reader,

This was a hard book to write. Everyone's story of grief is as individual as each person. The death of a child is not something a parent gets over. If this is your story, I'm so sorry this happened to your child, to you and to your family.

I lost a child to miscarriage, but I never experienced the kind of loss Jack and Kate suffered. I have tried to depict the pain of their journey with honesty, respect and love.

For a bereaved parent, the journey to healing is never complete. It will remain a lifelong pursuit. The circuitous path to peace is unique to each mother and father. I hope you will look kindly on my imperfect attempt to portray hope in the midst of such gut-wrenching anguish.

Thank you for sharing Jack, Kate and Liddy's story with me. For all of you, and especially to those who grieve, I pray for you the brightest of tomorrows, full of love, beauty and joy in that better, eternal garden.

I love hearing from readers so please contact me at lisa@lisacarterauthor.com or visit lisacarterauthor.com, where you can also subscribe to my e-newsletter.

In His Love,
Lisa Carter

COMING NEXT MONTH FROM
Love Inspired

HER AMISH ADVERSARY
Indiana Amish Market • by Vannetta Chapman

Bethany Yoder loves working at her father's outdoor Amish market, but when he hires Aaron King to help out, Bethany and Aaron don't see eye to eye about anything. She wants to keep things the same. He's all for change. Can opposites ever attract and turn to love?

THE AMISH BACHELOR'S BRIDE
by Pamela Desmond Wright

Amish widow Lavinia Simmons is shocked to learn that her late husband gambled away their home. Desperate to find a place for herself and her daughter, she impulsively accepts bachelor Noem Witzel's proposal. A marriage of convenience just might blend two families into one loving home.

DEPENDING ON THE COWBOY
Wyoming Ranchers • by Jill Kemerer

Rancher Blaine Mayer's life gets complicated when his high school crush, Sienna Powell, comes to stay with her niece and nephew for the summer. Recently divorced and six-months pregnant, Sienna takes his mind off his ranch troubles, but can he give her his heart, too?

BOUND BY A SECRET
Lone Star Heritage • by Jolene Navarro

After his wife's murder, Greyson McKinsey seeks a fresh start in Texas with his twin girls in the witness protection program. When he hires contractor Savannah Espinoza to restore his barns, his heart comes back to life. But can he ever trust her with the truth?

TOGETHER FOR THE TWINS
by Laurel Blount

When Ryder Montgomery assumes guardianship of his out-of-control twin nephews, he flounders. So he enlists the help of a professional nanny. Elise Cooper quickly wins the boys' hearts—and their uncle's admiration. One sweet summer might convince the perpetual bachelor to give love and family a try...

RESCUING HER RANCH
Stone River Ranch • by Lisa Jordan

Returning home after losing her job, Macey Stone agrees to care for the daughter of old friend Cole Crawford. When Macey discovers Cole is behind a land scheme that threatens Stone River Ranch, will she have to choose between her family's legacy and their newfound love?

LOOK FOR THESE AND OTHER LOVE INSPIRED BOOKS WHEREVER BOOKS ARE SOLD, INCLUDING MOST BOOKSTORES, SUPERMARKETS, DISCOUNT STORES AND DRUGSTORES.

LICNM1222

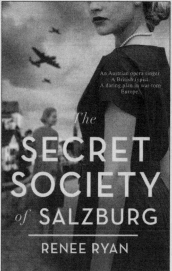

Get 4 FREE REWARDS!

We'll send you 2 FREE Books plus 2 FREE Mystery Gifts.

Both the **Love Inspired®** and **Love Inspired® Suspense** series feature compelling novels filled with inspirational romance, faith, forgiveness and hope.

YES! Please send me 2 FREE novels from the Love Inspired or Love Inspired Suspense series and my 2 FREE gifts (gifts are worth about $10 retail). After receiving them, if I don't wish to receive any more books, I can return the shipping statement marked "cancel." If I don't cancel, I will receive 6 brand-new Love Inspired Larger-Print books or Love Inspired Suspense Larger-Print books every month and be billed just $6.49 each in the U.S. or $6.74 each in Canada. That is a savings of at least 16% off the cover price. It's quite a bargain! Shipping and handling is just 50¢ per book in the U.S. and $1.25 per book in Canada.* I understand that accepting the 2 free books and gifts places me under no obligation to buy anything. I can always return a shipment and cancel at any time by calling the number below. The free books and gifts are mine to keep no matter what I decide.

Choose one: ☐ **Love Inspired**
Larger-Print
(122/322 IDN GRHK)

☐ **Love Inspired Suspense**
Larger-Print
(107/307 IDN GRHK)

Name (please print)

Address   Apt. #

City   State/Province   Zip/Postal Code

Email: Please check this box ☐ if you would like to receive newsletters and promotional emails from Harlequin Enterprises ULC and its affiliates. You can unsubscribe anytime.

Mail to the **Harlequin Reader Service:**
IN U.S.A.: P.O. Box 1341, Buffalo, NY 14240-8531
IN CANADA: P.O. Box 603, Fort Erie, Ontario L2A 5X3

Want to try 2 free books from another series? Call 1-800-873-8635 or visit www.ReaderService.com.

*Terms and prices subject to change without notice. Prices do not include sales taxes, which will be charged (if applicable) based on your state or country of residence. Canadian residents will be charged applicable taxes. Offer not valid in Quebec. This offer is limited to one order per household. Books received may not be as shown. Not valid for current subscribers to the Love Inspired or Love Inspired Suspense series. All orders subject to approval. Credit or debit balances in a customer's account(s) may be offset by any other outstanding balance owed by or to the customer. Please allow 4 to 6 weeks for delivery. Offer available while quantities last.

Your Privacy—Your information is being collected by Harlequin Enterprises ULC, operating as Harlequin Reader Service. For a complete summary of the information we collect, how we use this information and to whom it is disclosed, please visit our privacy notice located at corporate.harlequin.com/privacy-notice. From time to time we may also exchange your personal information with reputable third parties. If you wish to opt out of this sharing of your personal information, please visit readerservice.com/consumerschoice or call 1-800-873-8635. **Notice to California Residents**—Under California law, you have specific rights to control and access your data. For more information on these rights and how to exercise them, visit corporate.harlequin.com/california-privacy.

LIRLIS22R3

HARLEQUIN
PLUS

Announcing a **BRAND-NEW**
multimedia subscription service
for romance fans like you!

Read, Watch and Play.

Experience the easiest way to get
the romance content you crave.

Start your **FREE 7 DAY TRIAL** at
www.harlequinplus.com/freetrial.